Reptiles

BIG CA

Giraffe House

DON'T FEED THE BOY

DON'T FEED THE BOY

IRENE LATHAM

Illustrated by STEPHANIE GRAEGIN

ROARING BROOK PRESS
New York

Text copyright © 2012 by Irene Latham
Illustrations copyright © 2012 by Stephanie Graegin
Published by Roaring Brook Press
Roaring Brook Press is a division of
Holtzbrinck Publishing Holdings Limited Partnership
175 Fifth Avenue, New York, New York 10010
mackids.com

Library of Congress Cataloging-in-Publication Data

Latham, Irene.
   Don't feed the boy / Irene Latham ; illustrated by Stephanie Graegin.
—1st ed.
      p. cm.
   Summary: Eleven-year-old Whit's zookeeper parents have rarely allowed him
to go outside of the Alabama zoo they run, but he stops seeing it as such a cage
when he meets "Bird Girl," for whom the place is a refuge from problems at home.
   ISBN 978-1-59643-755-5 (hardcover)
   [1. Zoos—Fiction.   2. Zoo animals—Fiction.   3. Friendship—Fiction.
4. Family problems—Fiction.   5. Home schooling—Fiction.
6. Contentment—Fiction.]   I. Graegin, Stephanie, ill.   II. Title.
III. Title: Do not feed the boy.
   PZ7.L3476Don 2012
   [Fic]—dc23
                                                                2011047113

Roaring Brook Press books are available for special promotions and premiums.
For details contact: Director of Special Markets, Holtzbrinck Publishers.

First edition 2012
Book design by Roberta Pressel
Printed in the United States of America by RR Donnelley & Sons Company,
Harrisonburg, Virginia

10 9 8 7 6 5 4 3 2 1

For Andrew, Daniel & Eric–
my favorite species

1 ✳ FIELD STUDY

Whit waited for the toucan to turn its head before he stepped past the iron gate. He'd lived his whole life at the Meadowbrook Zoo, and until today he'd never disobeyed the three basic rules his parents set for him:

1. Don't feed the animals.
2. Schoolwork comes first.
3. Don't leave the zoo property for any reason.

He'd done everything that was expected of him. He hadn't fed the animals, even though Whit knew what treats they liked and had full access to the animal kitchens. He did all the reading and reports his home-school teacher, Ms. Connie, assigned, often ahead of schedule. And he had never even tried to leave the zoo, even though he was unattended much of the time and could have easily snuck away. And how he'd wanted to sneak away, especially in the past few months.

As he passed a family of four who were plotting how to hit all of the major animal shows in one visit, his legs resumed a more natural stride. He didn't dare look back at the gate. Because the gate would only remind him of the zoo rules, and if he thought about the rules, he might lose his courage. Better to let it all fade away: the rules, his parents, the gate, the animals.

Not that the exotic animals weren't interesting. They were fascinating. Some of them were even cute. But none of them made very good friends. And Whit was convinced that he was missing out on something important by spending his whole life stuck at the zoo. Or, *someone* important. Like the Bird Girl. If ever there was a reason to rewrite the rules, it was her.

As a line of dusty vehicles pulled into the zoo driveway, Whit turned toward the cluster of pine trees that marked the end of the parking lot and the beginning of the Picnic Pavilion. He could just see the Bird Girl claiming a spot at one of only two empty tables.

He took a deep breath. It seemed silly to him that his parents considered the Picnic Pavilion off-property. Technically it was still the zoo.

As he dodged sticky-fingered children on his way toward her, he pressed his lips together. That's the argument he would use if he got caught. Because off-property or not, Whit didn't care. He had to meet the Bird Girl. She had been coming to the zoo for six days in a row now. Six! He couldn't let another one pass without at least introducing himself.

He pushed his shoulders back. Walking up to someone and saying "Hi, my name is Whit" was only difficult because he so seldom had the opportunity to make new friends. Yes, he was surrounded by people every day, and his parents worked hard to provide "socialization" by inviting zoo employees to bring their families to the annual Spring Picnic and Holiday Gala and the Fall Apart Party that marked the end of the busy summer season. But that was only three times a year. And Whit was pretty sure *real* friendships were formed over daily rubbery hotdogs in the lunchroom or weekly sleepless sleepovers.

As he stood near the Bird Girl's table, he thought she was only the most interesting creature he had ever seen. She was different—that was clear from the very first day. For one thing, she always came alone. That all by itself was unusual. Most people came to the zoo with their families. And she always wore the same cut-off jeans and plain white T-shirt that draped almost to the edge of her shorts. Whit imagined it must belong to the missing father, or maybe a brother. Or maybe she just wasn't the kind of girl who cared about clothes.

He fumbled in his pocket for his digital recorder, glad that Ms. Connie had insisted he carry it with him for those "unexpected adventures" she got especially excited about. And the little machine really was handy. He pressed the green button and whispered, "June 8, 11:00 a.m." He remembered the morning's weather report on Channel 6. "Stage 2 drought. Subject tucks hair behind her ears and unzips backpack."

The recorder clicked as Whit took his finger off the button. A few minutes had passed and he was still successfully blending in with the guests. He glanced back toward the zoo gate, not exactly sure what he had expected would happen when he broke the rule. Alarm bells clanging? Zoo security rushing to collect him? He'd never imagined he could slip out so easily.

He drummed his fingers on the table. He didn't know what he was waiting for. The Bird Girl was right there, at the next table over. This was his chance. And instead of leaping across the table, he was mired in a strange sense of disappointment. He'd left the zoo, and no one had noticed. There should have been driving sheets of rain, booming thunder, and vibrant streaks of lightning. Heck, his disobedience should be enough to end the drought completely.

Instead, there wasn't a cloud in sight. Which put the count up to fifty-two days without rain. Not that the whole drought business mattered all that much to Whit. It was just part of his summer assignment.

"A field study," Ms. Connie said when she'd given him the instructions on the last day of May. "Pick any animal, any one you want. Think about the drought, how it affects the animal. Make a prediction. Then watch and record."

Whit grinned as the Bird Girl pulled a black note-book from the backpack. Ms. Connie may have been his teacher since he was four years old, but she'd still be impressed when she found out he'd picked a human instead of one of the 750 animals in the zoo collection. She was always encouraging him to get creative with his assignments. "Make it your own," she said. As if there was any other way.

Whit's fingers found the button on the recorder.

He was all for making the project fun. "Subject places notebook in lap, pulls out pencil pouch." He made his voice sound whispery and firm, like one of those golf sportscasters on TV. "I predict we will become friends."

His prediction didn't have a thing to do with the drought, but it was a start. The Bird Girl didn't seem to be affected by the drought at all. Come to think of it, neither did most of the animals at Meadowbrook Zoo. Probably because the staff worked so hard to keep the animals fed and watered. Even with current water usage restrictions, the landscaping staff somehow managed to keep the zoo grounds lush and attractive.

Whit held his breath as the Bird Girl folded back her sketch pad, opened her red pouch, and chose a fresh pencil. When she touched the pencil to the tip of her tongue, same as she had done every morning since the start of summer vacation, Whit's heart began to thump like a rabbit's foot.

Every day was the same. The Bird Girl started back inside the zoo at the bench in front of Flamingo Island. She watched for a while, and then she began to draw. Once that pencil touched the paper, it was like she wasn't even aware of anything else in the world. Every move seemed to have such purpose.

He held his hand over his mouth so no one would see or hear him talking into his recorder. "Subject appears to be drawing pigeons."

Pigeons. That was new. But it made sense, because the Picnic Pavilion was where those pudgy birds liked to hang out.

Unlike the animals inside the fence, guests could feed the pigeons. And they did, all the time. Whit's mother, who was a veterinarian before she became the zoo director, said those pigeons were getting so fat that soon they wouldn't even be able to fly. Not that they needed to with the corners of peanut butter and jelly sandwiches being thrust at them so many times a day.

Whit gripped his digital recorder as he dared move toward her table. As he settled onto the bench across from her, the Bird Girl shifted in her seat. Her head was no longer bent over the sketch pad. Instead it was like a scene in a movie, as if the camera had cut away for a second, and now it was back with a close-up shot that filled the screen. The Bird Girl's dark eyes were staring straight at him.

2 ❋ A NATURAL

"So, what are you watching me for?" she said, her voice calm, as if strange boys popped up in front of her every day.

Whit gasped and fumbled the digital recorder. Just as it was about to slide out of his hand and collide with the wooden tabletop, his fingers miraculously closed around it.

She pushed her hair back and spoke again before he was fully recovered. "Am I doing something wrong?" She unfolded herself from the bench. "I'll leave if the table is reserved or something."

Whit's face flushed as he looked down at his regulation green zoo staff shirt. Of course. She thought he worked there. He had the nametag and everything. "Um, no. It's not you." The last thing he wanted was for her to leave. "I mean, the tables aren't reserved. You can sit here if you want to."

She sank back down onto the seat, relief lifting her cheeks into a smile. "Thanks."

An interesting face, Whit thought. Hardy features sweetened by a faint sprinkling of freckles. Like she'd be good in a commercial for whole-grain cereal.

She moved the pencil with short, confident strokes. In no time at all the strokes became wings, and the wings became pigeons pecking the ground for bits of bread. She didn't seem to mind him watching her work. In fact, it seemed as if she'd forgotten him altogether.

Whit swallowed and broke the silence. "Do you take lessons?"

She shook her head but didn't look up from her sketch pad. "My mom says my father used to draw with me a long time ago. But I don't remember it."

"Wow. You're really good. Especially for not having lessons." Whit searched his mind for something else art related to add to the conversation. When he found it, his words came out in a rush. "You know Millie, the elephant?"

"Sure, everybody knows Millie."

"Well, she does art sometimes. You know, with a paintbrush in her trunk? And then we auction them off or sell them in the gift shop. My dad says she's a natural." He paused. "I think you're a natural, too."

The pencil stopped as the Bird Girl looked him in the eye. "A natural, huh?"

He waved toward her sketch pad. "Well, yeah. I've seen you here every day for nearly a week. All you do is draw."

Her eyes narrowed. "You've been watching me?" She flipped the cover over the sketch pad. "Every day?"

Oh no. Now why did he have to go and say a thing like that? She probably thought he was a stalker or something. "No, it's not like that," Whit said, his blush spreading to his scalp now, so he could almost feel the pinkness beneath his white-blond hair. "It's for my summer home-school project. A field study. I could have picked any of the animals, but they do the same thing at the same time every day. You—you're different."

She rolled her eyes. "If you've been watching me for a week, then you know that's not true." She thumbed the pages of her sketch pad, allowing him a glimpse of her work. "See? All birds. Every day I draw birds."

"Well, they *are* amazing creatures," Whit said, eager to change the subject. And yes, he had noticed. Of course he had noticed. But better not to say that now. Now was the time to be cool and witty, the way he'd seen boys on TV. "Not as cool as the giraffes, but still amazing."

"Giraffes, huh?" She tapped her pencil against the paper, as if she was seriously pondering what he had said. Or maybe she was just pondering him.

Whit couldn't say for sure. And it didn't really matter, because he was entranced. He couldn't stop staring, even though he knew it was rude. He wanted to tell her that what he'd said about the giraffes wasn't just a lame effort at making conversation. Of all the animals in the zoo, the giraffes were Whit's favorite. They were proof that you didn't have to be flashy or noisy to be popular. Just really, *really* tall.

But he was afraid to say all that. So he just stuck with the facts. "Yep, they're quiet animals. Even when they're hungry or scared. They don't make a peep."

The Bird Girl sighed. "I'll have to tell my brother you said that. He says being quiet can be a good survival method."

Whit nodded, encouraged by her words. "They also have a really sweet smell. Not like the other animals."

"Well—" she chuckled "—one thing my brother does *not* have is a really sweet smell."

Whit's armpits started to itch. He sure hoped that *he* hadn't started to smell. "So you have a brother. What's that like?"

The pigeons cooed as they searched the ground for crumbs and Whit watched the sweeping movement of the Bird Girl's pencil as she shaped another set of wings. "I don't know. He's been gone to Mobile for almost a year now. I can hardly remember what it's like."

Whit drew his brows together. Mobile was like four hours away. "What, is he in college or something?"

The Bird Girl shook her head. "No. He ran away. He lives on his own now."

"Why did he run away?" The words tumbled out of Whit's mouth as his heart jumped in his chest like one of those old-fashioned alarm clocks that bounces as it rings. Then he ground his teeth together before he could say anything else stupid. It was rude to ask a person why. If they wanted you to know, they'd tell you. Besides, *why* was such a useless question anyway. He'd listened to his parents waste whole days on *why*. They'd spin theory after theory on animal behavior and why some animals thrived in captivity and others didn't. You could make a million guesses and every one of them was liable to be wrong.

Before he could apologize, the Bird Girl answered. "Same reason I'm going to run away. To get away from my father."

A droplet of sweat slid down the side of Whit's face. As he swiped it away with the back of his hand, he wasn't sure what to say. Hadn't she just said her father used to do art with her? That didn't sound like someone you'd want to run away from. He decided humor was probably the safest response. "You should meet *my* father. He knows so much about elephants he might as well *be* one. And he already has the ears." Whit flapped his hands at the sides of his head.

When she didn't laugh, or even smile, Whit knew he'd blown it. Her mouth was all drawn up and her brow was wrinkled as she pressed her pencil to the page and concentrated on sketching the pigeon's beak. The way she hunched over the sketchbook reminded Whit of the ground guineas. Whenever the mother guinea felt threatened, she would throw her wings over the chicks making them invisible to predators.

As he scrambled for what to say next, a frantic voice called from behind them. "Whit, there you are!"

It was Ms. Connie. Her cheeks were red and short tendrils of hair curled around her face. Whit realized she'd probably been racing all over the place looking for him. She'd probably been worried sick.

He shot out of his seat. "Hi, Ms. Connie. I was just working on my project."

"But you're not supposed to be out here, Whit. You know that! Vivian would be furious if she knew."

Vivian was his mother. And *furious* was the perfect word. When his mother gave an order, she expected it to be carried out. Vivian would be as angry with Ms. Connie as she was with Whit.

"I'm sorry, Ms. Connie." She may have been hired by his mother, but his teacher was almost always on Whit's side. Thank goodness his parents trusted her so completely. If it hadn't been for her all these years, he was sure he wouldn't know anything about the world outside the Meadowbrook Zoo.

He glanced at the Bird Girl who was watching

intently. "I just—" He had no idea how to explain. "Everything's okay. I'm right here."

Ms. Connie looked from Whit to the Bird Girl and back again. Then she lightly touched Whit's arm. "Thank goodness." She took a deep breath. "But you have to say goodbye, Whit." Her tone was tender now that the scare was over, and she offered the Bird Girl a smile. "Anytime you want to visit Whit, you're absolutely welcome." She paused. "But without my supervision, it has to be inside the zoo. We can't have Whit running around like a wild animal. It wouldn't be safe."

As irritated as he was to be pulled away like a pre-schooler, Whit was grateful for Ms. Connie's kindness. If it had been Vivian who had found them it would have been a whole different scene. "Bye," he said and offered a stiff wave.

"Bye, Whit," the Bird Girl said, her voice lilting, like a song.

Whit grinned back and thought how nice his name sounded coming out of her mouth. Whatever he'd said wrong before seemed to be forgotten. She looked at him as if they were friends.

Whit's mind turned with possibility as he and Ms. Connie made their way back through the front gate.

He resisted the urge to skip as he replayed the whole encounter. He'd actually talked to her. And better yet, he'd done okay. He decided that he didn't regret a single moment. Except for one thing: He still didn't have a clue what *her* name was. But he was sure going to find out.

3 ✳ THE BENCH BESIDE FLAMINGO ISLAND

The next day Whit woke up thinking about the Bird Girl. Ms. Connie promised she wouldn't mention the incident at the Picnic Pavilion to his parents, so long as he promised not to do it again. Of course Whit promised. Now that the Bird Girl knew he existed, it shouldn't matter so much. They could just talk at the zoo, inside the gate.

As he dressed and brushed his teeth, he decided the first thing he would do when he saw her was ask her about her name. He knew he couldn't keep calling her the Bird Girl, not if they were really going to be friends. He needed to know her actual name. It was probably something substantial sounding with a lot of syllables, like John James Audubon. Except for a girl.

He was sure it wouldn't be anything like his own one-syllable name. Whit. Where was the creativity, the enthusiasm in a name like that? It didn't even mean anything, the way most of the zoo animals' names did. Like Millie the elephant, whose name may sound common enough but actually was short for Millicent, which means "brave strength." And Whit's name sure hadn't been carefully selected from hoards of suggestions sent in by little kids and teachers the way it happened when the zoo got a new chimpanzee or Siberian tiger. It was just further proof that his parents preferred the animals and would rather be naming exotic species than anything else.

Whit had heard the story a thousand times. It was his parents' third trip to Africa. Along with the two white rhinos they helped capture, they brought home a bad case of dysentery and a tiny bunch of cells that would eventually become Whit. As soon as his mother found out she was pregnant, she eliminated caffeine and sushi from her diet and piped Mozart through headphones attached to her stomach. She followed the latest scientific advice so that her baby was sure to be healthy. But the truth was, they never wanted to be parents.

"What a surprise you were!" Whit's mother liked to say. Then her eyes would get all fuzzy and she'd drift away again, her attention drawn to the computer screen and its Red List of Endangered Animals. Or the Species Survival Plan for the red panda. How could he possibly compete with that? It wasn't Whit's fault he happened to be born the wrong species.

But there wasn't any point in dwelling on it. Especially not when the Bird Girl was probably out there in the zoo, waiting for him already. And instead of his own boring stories, he could find out more about her. Not just her name, but everything. Like why her brother ran away, and what the problem was with her father, and why she liked to draw birds. He had so many questions he wanted to ask her.

He found her at the bench beside Flamingo Island, the same place he'd seen her every day so far. She was drawing. And for just a minute, Whit wasn't sure he wanted to interrupt her. It was such a perfect scene.

The flamingos, for their part, were doing exactly what they and all the other animals did every morning, no matter what the weather: watching as the first guests of the day trickled through the front gate.

Whit dragged his eyes away from the Bird Girl and surveyed the sprawling zoo. It was his favorite moment of the whole day, when the first families walked in and the air changed instantly from prickly anticipation to a sigh of peace and calm. Drought or no drought, the animals needed the guests to come. They were accustomed to being pointed at and stared at and got upset when they weren't getting enough attention.

The part no one understood unless they were at the zoo every single day was how monotonous it could be. And that's exactly how the animals liked it.

He watched a father unfold a zoo map while the mother fumbled through the bags hanging from the handle of the big-wheeled jogging stroller, no doubt looking for Goldfish crackers or a juice box.

Whit could see it all happening from his secret spot beside the Reptile House. And even though they knew nothing about him, Whit knew just how the day would go for this family and the next. How the now-sparkling children dressed in their hats and bows and little white sandals, would, by the end of the day, morph into juice-stained, one-shoed, sunburned, grumpy little people who needed their nap, but didn't know how to say "I need my nap," so they simply screamed and threw things instead.

Yep, it was all so predictable. Which is why his

stomach buzzed with excitement as he approached the Bird Girl. But before he could get there, his father came around the corner of the Reptile House.

"Mornin', son."

Whit forced his voice to sound normal when he said hello, even though his heart pounded in his ears. He hadn't been expecting his father. Yet, there he was in clownish blue coveralls with a bright yellow nametag shouting "Tony Whitaker, Head Elephant Keeper." In one hand he held a push broom.

"Don't you have lessons today?" He leaned against the broom. "I thought your mother said you were going to be in the Primate House this morning."

Whit nodded. The Primate House was exactly where he was supposed to be. And his father was all about schedules because of his work with the elephants. Which is why Whit hated to bother him with stuff. He could have explained to Tony what animal he'd chosen for his summer field study project, but it was easier just *not* to. Instead, he fell back on a familiar complaint, guaranteed to generate a familiar answer. "It's not fair," Whit said, thinking fast. "All the other kids get off for summer vacation."

Tony chuckled. "All the other kids?" He set the

broom between his feet and held it there with his knee-high rubber boots. "All the other kids have to sit at desks five days a week while you get your very own teacher just three days a week. And the rest of the time, the entire zoo is your playground!" He swung his arms wide. "Now you tell me who's got the better deal."

Whit waited for him to launch into his speech about how lucky Whit was to grow up in a zoo. How when he was a kid money was so tight that his family only ever got to go to the zoo on the one day of the year when they offered free admission. And that day was always so thick with people that you could hardly see the animals at all.

But his father didn't say any of that. And he didn't say the part about how fortunate Whit was to grow up without any worries about money. How his whole generation was spoiled. How they didn't have any idea how good they had it.

Those kinds of speeches were another reason why Whit didn't talk much to his father. Tony hardly gave him a chance. Which was something of an improvement over the way Vivian flat-out ignored him, but still. Tony's favorite conversations were about one of two things: the elephants or himself. He loved to tell the story about when he was a teenager and worked as a clown in the City Circus. How all he'd ever wanted was to be was an elephant keeper, and how grateful he was to get paid to work with the animals he loved best. It made Whit want to throw up.

Tony tousled Whit's hair. "Or you could come with me." He hoisted the broom again to his shoulder and headed down the walk. "It's been a while since you visited my girls."

Whit shook his head. He'd rather go to the Primate House than the Elephant House any day. At least the primates acted a little bit like people.

If only he loved the elephants the way his father did, life would be so much easier. Because it was true: Everybody loved Millie, the matriarch, and her two daughters Wanda and Lila. Of all the animals, those three elephants got more newspaper and TV coverage than all the rest put together. Whit never had understood it. Sure they were huge, and it was amazing what they could do with those trunks. But it wasn't like you could cuddle up with them. And of all the animals, they were most likely to kill you.

Whit couldn't count the number of close calls his

father had experienced. Just a month ago Tony made the mistake of getting between Millie and the wall of the enclosure. In a matter of seconds Millie began to lean against him, putting on more pressure with each passing second. If Tony hadn't dropped to the ground, she would have crushed him for sure.

But Tony didn't hold that against her. There wasn't a thing any one of those elephants could do to change his mind about them. He'd been with Millie for twenty years. And the babies—Wanda for ten years and Lila for four.

Tony whisked the broom toward Whit, as if sweeping him in the direction of the Primate House.

"I'm going," Whit said. He waited for his father to turn the corner before dashing over to the Bird Girl. He didn't have time to explain everything about the zoo rules, but he thought he should at least say hello.

The Bird Girl beat him to it. "Look who it is."

His words tumbled through the air. "I wish I could stay, but I can't." He took a breath. "But I can meet you here tomorrow. I mean, if you want to."

She jiggled her pencil, as if deciding. "Okay," she said finally.

Relief loosened all of Whit's muscles. As he waved goodbye and loped toward the Primate House, his grin was so wide it made his eyes squint.

He'd talked to her again. Without messing it up. And he didn't need Ms. Connie's expertise on the outside world to know that *okay* pretty much always means *yes*.

4 ❧ MAKE A WISH

The next day Whit met Ms. Connie at the Primate House a whole hour earlier than usual. She lifted an eyebrow as though she knew he was up to something but didn't ask any questions. Instead she consulted her clipboard, which held the list of assignments for all the required subjects. "Today we'll be discussing animal reproduction in captivity." She handed Whit a little cardboard wheel gadget that was about as big as his palm.

"What's this?" He recognized the name printed on the wheel. It was the company that Vivian bought the horsemeat from. Horsemeat, for the lions.

Ms. Connie smiled. "Spin it. You'll see."

Whit spun the little wheel with his thumb. When it stopped turning, the arrow pointed to "lemur." And in the tiny window, it read "132–134 days."

"Wow." He spun the wheel again. "That's how long it takes for a lemur to develop before it's born?"

Ms. Connie nodded. "We could have done this lesson with one of Vivian's dusty, old textbooks, but I figured you'd like the wheel."

He grinned and thanked her. He was in such a good mood that he even stuck around after the lesson to help the keepers measure out monkey chow for the macaques—a chore he usually avoided because it took up so much time. But he knew the keepers would send word to his mother. She would be so pleased by his unsolicited help that she wouldn't keep tabs on him. He would have the rest of the day to fully concentrate on the Bird Girl.

By the time Whit got back to Flamingo Island, it was mid-morning and the walkways had begun to get crowded. He wiped his hands across his khaki pants and hoped that they didn't smell like the monkey chow, which was sort of like dry dog food. Not horrible, but still potentially embarrassing. He didn't want anything to mess up his time with the Bird Girl.

"Let me guess," he said as he approached the bench where the Bird Girl had taken up her usual perch.

He'd planned this part out so well that his voice actually came out without a quaver. "You're drawing flamingos again."

She shielded her eyes to look at him. "And you're watching me again."

When she smiled, Whit knew she wasn't upset or anything. He was so relieved that he momentarily forgot the part he had planned to say next. His breath caught and his eyes widened. The words were just gone.

He scrambled for something, anything that would make sense. "In the wild," Whit said finally and cleared his throat. "In the wild their feathers would be a deeper pink." Whit clasped his hands behind his back to keep himself from making any odd gestures.

"I know," she said and turned her attention to the flamingos. "I learned that in school." She brought the pencil to her mouth again, this time bouncing the eraser off her bottom lip as Whit shifted his weight from one leg to the other.

"Really? What school?"

"Meadowbrook. I'll go to the middle school next year."

"Wow. What's that like?"

She laughed and pointed at the flamingos, some of which were milling around, some preening, others digging around in the shallow water for food. "Pretty much like that. Minus the pink."

Whit grinned. "It's more of a salmon color, really." He couldn't remember a time when conversation about zoo animals had been so much fun.

"Because of all the shrimp they eat, right?"

Whit nodded, and they were both quiet while inside the enclosure one of the larger flamingos bullied its way past three other smaller flamingos, nipping them until they squawked and jumped out of the way.

When the birds settled, Whit sat down on the bench beside her. "So what's your name anyway? I can't keep calling you 'the Bird Girl.'"

She grinned shyly. "You can call me Bird Girl if you want to." Then she held out her hand. "Or my real name. Stella."

Stella. It was perfect for her. And he felt so grown up shaking her hand, although at the same time it seemed a little odd. Did kids really do that with each other? The fact that his hand was sweaty didn't help, either. Especially when her hand was so small in his, so delicate. It reminded him of the Butterfly Tent Vivian put up every spring. How you'd walk in and the butterflies would flutter their wings, all grace and light, then land on a flower as if weightless. It didn't even feel quite real.

They separated and Whit resisted the urge to wipe his hand on his pants. It was embarrassing enough watching Stella wipe hers.

"So, Stella." He liked the way the word tasted in his mouth. Then, just like he'd seen in a documentary about Billy the Kid, he lifted an imaginary cowboy hat and cut the air in a gallant, sweeping gesture. "The Meadowbrook Zoo awaits." He'd always wanted someone to try that with.

Stella's reaction was equally as dramatic as she pressed her hand to her heart and batted her eyelids. Clearly they'd seen the same program. She hadn't made him feel foolish at all, the way he'd imagined someone might. She'd just played right along. He thought she was perfect.

While Stella packed up her art supplies, Whit decided to take her to see the giraffes. It would give him plenty of time to find out more about her. "You must live close by," he said.

She nodded. "You know that row of apartments just past the Botanical Gardens?"

He didn't. But the Botanical Gardens were just across the street from the zoo, so he knew it wasn't far. "So you just walk over?"

She waited as a man snapped a shot of a woman posed in front of the Bear Country sign. "I don't walk. I don't even run. I *fly*." She grinned. "I'd rather be here than at home." That explained why she had been at the zoo so many days in a row. And it brought up more questions, too. Questions Whit wasn't quite ready to ask.

He resumed his role as Billy the Kid. "Glad to be of service, ma'am." He tipped his imaginary hat. "We aim to please." The Kid may have been an outlaw, but he was generally polite. Whit knew that from the DVD.

When she giggled, Whit did his best cowboy swagger. He couldn't believe how easy the conversation was, even when they had to dodge some of the other guests. If they got separated, they would pause, then pick right back up when they were together again. After so many days watching her just sit on the bench, he liked to watch her move. Her stride was sure and confident, and Whit could tell just by the way she walked that the Bird Girl wasn't one of those people who got bored when the monkeys weren't doing anything. She didn't seem in a hurry at all, and she even stopped to read the signs posted outside the turtle exhibit. Pretty much nobody read past the part that identified the animals. All the extra stuff about habitat and diet and mating habits? Most guests didn't have time for that. They wanted the animals to *do* something. And if they didn't, the guests complained.

Whit wished he could make everyone who visited the zoo understand that the animals didn't have a clue how to entertain. That's why Whit's mother brought in the carousel and the ice-cream cart—and the train that whistled and chugged and cost two dollars per person, thank you very much.

As they passed the entrance to the newest exhibit, Whit couldn't help telling Stella all about it. After all, it had been the suppertime topic at his house for three straight years. The zoo had named it Savannah Point. What made it special was how the clever design allowed you to see lions, zebras, and giraffes all at once. As if you really were in Africa instead of a mid-sized zoo in central Alabama. Whit knew Savannah Point was the closest most of the guests would ever get to Africa.

"Ever been to Africa?" he asked Stella. Her answer

was put on hold as three rambunctious boys pushed between them in their rush to see the turtle exhibit. Their mother trailed behind them, apologizing as she passed. Once the boys were gone, Whit pointed out to Stella the four turtles that were sunning themselves on one of the strategically placed logs, their necks stretched toward the sky. There were two more turtles, somewhere. Probably they were hiding behind the heart-shaped rock Whit's mother had placed at the back of the enclosure. No matter how much the keepers coaxed them with treats and enrichment toys, some of the animals were just private by nature.

"So, Africa," Whit said, returning to the subject. She shook her head, still looking at the turtles. "Anywhere else besides Alabama?" he asked.

She shook her head again. "You?"

He laughed. "Heck, no. But my parents have been on lots of trips. They've visited thirteen African countries so far."

"Where do you stay when they go?"

"Here. At the zoo. Usually Ms. Connie stays with me."

"Wow. Your teacher is your babysitter, too? I've never heard of that before."

"Well," he sputtered, "I wouldn't say babysitter." Although she had babysat for him when he was a toddler. "Teacher. She's my *teacher*. She's been with us so long she's practically one of the family." He paused to throw a pebble into the turtle pond. It was always hard for him to describe Ms. Connie. She was so much more than just a teacher or family friend.

Stella leaned over the stone wall to get a closer look at the turtles. "I have a bunch of family. In Mobile. Fourteen cousins."

Whit remembered what she'd said about her brother running away to Mobile. It made more sense if there was family there, too. "So do you go down there a lot? To visit?"

She tossed another pebble and waited for the plunk before speaking. "I wish. I really miss Hugo." She looked at him sideways. "You kind of remind me of him. He talks a lot, too."

Whit's eyes widened. He *had* been talking a lot. "It's just so great to have someone who talks back."

She pushed against him with her shoulder and laughed. "What about Ms. Connie? I bet she talks back."

He laughed. His teacher was definitely a talker. "Yes, but she's a grown-up."

"Hugo says just because someone's a grown-up doesn't mean they know what they're doing. He says you've got to watch out for number one. Make your own choices."

He shrugged, not really sure how they'd gotten from Ms. Connie to her brother's opinions about grown-ups. "Well, how old is he? There aren't a whole lot of choices you can make when you're eleven."

"True," she conceded and a silence fell between them as Stella swung her arms and Whit thought about his parents. All those times they'd gone to Africa without him, had they known what they were doing? He flashed back to tearful conversations when he complained about never getting to go anyplace different. "It's a business trip," his mother would explain. "We won't have any time to entertain you." Like his parents did such a great job of entertaining him at home. They just assumed he liked the zoo as much as they did. They never once asked.

Stella sat on the edge of the turtle pond and pulled a penny from her pocket. "Let's make a wish."

"Okay," Whit said. "You first."

"No." She handed him a penny. "We do it together. But we can't tell each other, because then the wish won't come true."

Whit's shoulders slumped. He wanted to know her wish. And he wanted to tell her his. But he could see by the way she was squeezing her eyes shut that to her, this was serious business. And if that's what she thought—well, a friend wouldn't argue with that. A friend would just squeeze his eyes shut, too.

Just before his penny plopped in the water, Whit tried to imagine what a girl like Stella would wish for. And just before he tossed his own penny into the water, he decided some day, if he ever got the chance, he would ask her. He wouldn't be like his parents and just assume things about her. He would actually ask until he got an answer.

Then he made his own wish. He wanted out. Out of the zoo. Away from this world that belonged to his parents, not to him. He wanted to find his thing the way his mother had found hers, back when she was a little girl visiting the zoo with her grandmother. He wanted to be *that* sure of something. He wanted to go to Meadowbrook Middle School with Stella, say hello to her in the halls. He wanted friends that weren't caged animals. Friends who would pay attention to him the same way he paid attention to them.

Whit could feel Stella watching him as he made his wish. He hoped she could tell it wasn't a joke to him. His whole life he had never wanted anything more.

Finally, he opened his eyes. "Done." He glanced at his watch. "Now let's go see the pelicans. It's just about time for the show."

5 ✳ PELICAN PLAZA

Every day at 10:30 a.m. and 2:30 p.m., it was feeding time at Pelican Plaza. Barry the pelican keeper would come out to the little dock that was supposed to look just like it came from New Orleans and toss fish from a metal bucket to the waiting pelicans.

They were a pair of brown pelicans, named Napoleon and Josephine. Whenever Barry walked out with his bucket they would rise from their flimsy ground nest of sticks and reeds and flap their wings. Then, as soon as Barry threw some fish into the water, they lifted their heavy bodies into the air and dove for it.

Whit moved his mouth along with Barry's as he continued the show. "The brown pelican's eyes are bigger than its stomach—or rather, its pouch is bigger than its stomach. See Napoleon's beak? It can hold up to three gallons but his stomach can only hold one."

Stella giggled. "You know all the words?"

Whit beamed. He'd always thought it was kind of sad that he knew the whole routine. As though it said something about how boring his life must be for him to have memorized Barry's entire speech. But Stella's reaction made him feel like it was special and important. "It's just what happens when you live in a zoo."

Her smile faded. "The only thing I've got memorized is my dad's rants. But they're pretty short."

"What? What does he say?"

She pressed her lips together and crossed her arms. Like she wanted to tell him something, but the words didn't taste good, so she was holding them back. Finally, she shook her head. "Not yet."

He clenched his jaw and replayed his own words in his head. Why did he have to be so eager, so pushy? Why did he have to rush in with all the questions? Clearly, her father was a sore spot. She already said her brother ran away because of him. It must be something really bad.

But she had said "yet" as if she was planning to tell him at some point.

"I'm going to the restroom," she mumbled. As she walked away, Whit thought this whole making conversation business was harder than it seemed. At first their talk had been going really well. And then . . . and then . . . it just died.

He leaned against the railing as Barry put down the microphone and stowed the fish bucket. He watched for Stella to emerge from the bathroom, but it was taking a while. He turned his wrist to check the time. 11:15. He drew his brows together and decided to pull out the digital recorder. "Subject agitated. Cause unknown." He thought he should say more. But he wasn't sure what.

Besides, now *he* was starting to get agitated. It wasn't his fault the conversation had stalled. But that didn't stop him from wanting to fix it.

As the June sun shot daggers into his shoulders and the top of his head, Whit ran his hands through his hair. What was taking her so long?

"Subject no longer visible. In restroom adjacent to Pelican Plaza." He checked his watch again. 11:20. She'd been in there for five minutes. He didn't know if he should be worried or just be more patient.

Distraction, that's what he needed. He looked across the sidewalk into Lorikeet Landing. He searched for their small blue heads and lime green wings, but they were high in the branches of the crape myrtle tree, too busy chattering with one another to be seen. All it would take was a small cup of nectar to bring the birds down, but Whit didn't want to enter the walk-in enclosure and risk losing track of the Bird Girl. She had to come out sometime.

Whit scanned the long sidewalk and the wooded area beside it where Ferdinand the peacock usually liked to stride along on sunny days, as if he was the lone sheriff of some dusty goldrush town. But Ferdinand was nowhere to be seen.

Whit crossed his arms and leaned against the smooth rock wall of the Reptile House. At least it was cool here in his secret spot. He closed his eyes and lifted his shoulders once, then set them back down.

What now? His neck was so tense. And it felt awkward just standing there, all silent and waiting. Next time Ms. Connie asked him to fill out one of those interests and aptitude surveys to find out what he wanted to study next he was going to write in something like "Bathroom Habits of Girls." If only he knew what was normal, he wouldn't be so concerned.

He scanned the perimeter again and could see the mom from the turtle pond, chasing after her three little boys. They were now just dots in the distance as they walked toward Bear Country. Whit looked over his shoulder again toward the restrooms, and his breath quickened.

Still, no Stella. Cruising down the walkway was Whit's father, broomless, and his face set in a scowl. As if he was the only person in the zoo.

Which meant something was going on. And it wasn't good.

He fought the impulse to duck back into the shadows and avoid Tony completely. But he'd learned from experience that it helped to know what was going on with his parents. That way he could better plot his strategy for how to deal with them. Ms. Connie would call it "being prepared."

He ground his teeth together. At least it would give him something to do while he waited for Stella.

6 ❋ ELEPHANT HOUSE

"Dad, wait," Whit called.

Tony rushed past him, barely acknowledging his son with a tight wave.

Weird, Whit thought, as he ran to catch up to him. "What's wrong?"

Tony's voice was gruff, and he didn't slow. "Not now, son. We'll talk later."

Whit stopped abruptly as Tony continued on. Was the schedule so important that he couldn't stop, just for a second, and tell his own son whatever it was that had made him so tense?

And then he heard Stella's voice. "That's your dad?" He spun around to find her standing right in front of him as if she hadn't been gone a second.

Whit nodded. He felt silly now for worrying about

her. She'd only gone to the restroom, for goodness' sake. Sometimes Ms. Connie took a long time in there, too. Still, his heart pounded with relief.

"Yep," he said finally, and forced himself to just breathe. He needed to quit second-guessing everything he said and just be himself. He couldn't exactly expect her to trust him if he didn't trust her. "He's the head elephant keeper."

The Bird Girl shifted her backpack from one shoulder to the other. "No way!" She took a long look at Whit, as if she were resizing him again, and grinned.

"Yep," Whit said, when he realized she wasn't disbelieving, just enthralled. He spent so little time outside of the zoo; it always surprised him when people acted like it was a big deal. "But don't be too impressed." Whit pushed down his anger at his father and focused on Stella. "By the end of the day, you can *smell* him coming."

The Bird Girl giggled, and Whit's whole body flushed. It felt so good to make someone laugh. Like he was a superhero or something.

Once they'd both quieted, Stella continued. "I'm sure Millie and Wanda and Lila like him just the way he is."

Now it was Whit's turn to be impressed. "You know all their names?" Most folks stumbled after "Millie."

"What, you think all I care about are the flamingos?"

Whit grinned. She was teasing him.

"You said yourself it's the only thing you draw. And in the past week, not once have I seen you at the Elephant House." Whit folded his arms across his chest. "Believe me," he said, his voice softer now, "if you'd been there, I'd know about it."

"The problem with elephants is they're so big. I'd run out of pencils."

Whit agreed with her one hundred percent. "And elephants are boring old gray. Birds get all the color." He decided to leave out the part about how deceiving all those vibrant feathers were. Birds in the zoo couldn't even fly. Every single one of the uncaged birds had their wings clipped.

Stella walked over to the enclosure that held the scarlet ibises. The two birds walked daintily through the tall grass, their curved beaks poking around for bits of crab and shrimp, the tips of their scarlet feathers gleaming black. "Hugo's the reason I draw birds." She tapped the bridge of her nose. "He said I already have a beak, so now all I need is wings."

Whit examined her profile. Her nose was kind of large, but it suited her. "I think you have a great nose. Not as great as mine, but still pretty great."

He forced himself not to flinch when she turned to look at his nose. He was a little self-conscious about it, even though Ms. Connie had assured him that the nose was often the first facial feature to grow during puberty and that his body would grow into it eventually.

Stella grabbed his chin to turn his head for an alternate view. "My mom says a big nose means good luck. So I guess we're both lucky, huh."

"Very lucky," he teased.

The conversation continued as they ambled down the sidewalk. She talked a lot about Hugo and how she hated being inside her house without him there to make her feel safe. Whit listened and said "uh-huh" but otherwise didn't interrupt her. He was so honored that she chose to confide in him. And when she grabbed his arm and said, "Your turn," he thought it was just the way he had imagined it would be like to have real friend. Listening *and* talking. It was so much better than the snorts and grunts and squawks he got from the animals.

He told her all about living at the zoo. How his parents were so busy with the animals that sometimes he had to look in a mirror just to prove to himself that he really did exist. Whit liked it that she was a good listener, too. And she didn't scold him the way his parents might. She also didn't rush in to fix things, which could be equally as annoying. He thought she was pretty much the perfect friend, even if she was a girl.

When they got to the Elephant House, his father was exactly where Whit expected him to be—in the runway with a hose in his hand. It was a demanding job to handle the mounds of waste produced by three elephants during a normal day. And Whit could tell by the pungent odor that this day wasn't normal. They always smelled, but it wasn't usually as strong as this.

And the mood was all wrong. Someone had turned the music way up, which Whit knew meant the keepers were having conversations they didn't want the guests to overhear. Tony's face was set in a scowl, and he wasn't paying any attention to the guests lined up along the enclosure.

Whit motioned to Stella. "Come on."

As they made their way around the back of the building, Whit watched one little girl pinch her nose. "Mommy, Millie stinks," she said, and pressed her face into her mother's leg. He had a feeling the smell had everything to do with Tony's mood.

When they came to a door that said "Zoo Employees Only," Whit quickly keyed in the numbered code and pushed open the door.

Stella hesitated. "Are you sure it's okay?"

Whit wasn't sure. The truth was, the issue had never come up. Because he'd never attempted to bring anyone else through that door. Even at the spring picnic two years ago when one of the older boys tried to bribe him with a bag of those malted robin's egg candies, he had refused. It was too personal.

But Whit had watched his parents bring visitors tons of times. They even brought the mayor back here once. And a little girl from the Make-A-Wish Foundation. Whit knew he wasn't putting Stella in danger or anything. And his parents had never said not to bring anyone back. It just had never happened before. So he just nodded his head and Stella followed.

As the door came to a close behind them, Tony lifted his eyebrows and cut off the stream of water.

"Whit? You need something?"

"No, just showing Stella around." Whit forced himself to hold Tony's gaze. As if he brought friends into the Elephant House every single day.

"Not such a good day for backstage visitors, I'm afraid." Tony wiped his brow with his arm. "Millie stood without sleeping the whole night last night. And now she's got a bad case of diarrhea. Doc's coming around directly to see what's the matter."

Whit's eyes widened. Doc was the staff veterinarian. And while Whit didn't love the elephants the way Tony did, he did care what happened to them. For Doc to stop his regular rounds and come *directly*— that was saying something. Doc was about as attached to his schedule as Tony was.

And Whit knew it was never good news when an elephant didn't sleep. Usually they would lie down for three or four hours at night. A standing elephant was a sure sign of sickness. Though it wasn't nearly as bad as an elephant that lay down and refused to get up. Whenever that happened, one had to be prepared for the worst news. All that weight put unnatural pressure on the lungs and would block the digestive tract. An elephant that doesn't stand, dies.

He swallowed. At least Millie was still standing. But he didn't say it out loud because he didn't want to say anything that might set Tony off. His father could be a bit unpredictable when the elephants were sick. "What about Wanda and Lila? They look fine."

Tony nodded. "You're right. We should be glad it's just Millie."

"Does Mom know?"

Tony shook his head. "She's in a board meeting, so I left her a message."

Whit rolled his eyes. His mom had been in a meeting the time he had croup and his throat got so tight he couldn't breathe. And the time he slipped on the concrete outside the Predator House and needed an X-ray. And the time his knees finally learned not to buckle when he strapped on roller skates. Of course she was in a meeting.

"Board meeting?" Stella said, her brows creased in confusion.

Whit scrambled to explain. "My mom is the director of the zoo."

"No way," she said. "The director? I knew she worked here, but wow. No wonder you know so much about animals. It's probably in your DNA."

Whit nodded and flashed a smile, happy to have impressed her again. "Hey, Dad, mind if me and Stella feed Lila her snack?"

"Stella, huh?" Tony said, like he hadn't heard Whit the first time he said her name. And Whit knew he probably hadn't. Then he pointed toward a bucket brimming with apples and carrots. "Sure, Whit. You know the rules."

Whit nodded. The rule was, of course, don't feed the animals. Except when he was accompanied by a keeper and under direct supervision. Any other time and he would get in big trouble.

As Tony turned back to the task of hosing off the floor, Whit realized his father hadn't asked a single other question about Stella. It bugged him that it was the first time he had brought another person behind the scenes—and a girl no less—yet Tony had nothing to say about it. Whit shouldn't have been surprised, but he was. His parents were predictable in all the wrong ways.

Stella watched as Whit retrieved a bucket from the long line of hooks. "So how do we do this?"

"Don't get too close," he instructed. "Let Lila do all the work. It's good for her to stretch. Safer, too." Whit relaxed his fingers and held out the apple in his flattened palm. "That trunk is composed of tens of thousands of muscles. Lila here can pick up a penny with that trunk. Or pull a tree right out of the ground."

Stella grabbed a carrot and held it out to Lila. Her eyes widened as Lila curled her trunk around it and pulled the carrot from her hand. "It tickles."

Whit grabbed an apple in each hand. "Lila's got a light touch. Dad says she has the sweetest disposition of any elephant he's ever seen." Whit leaned over and whispered in Stella's ear. "He likes to take credit for it. As if he's her father or something."

Stella offered Lila an apple. "Lucky elephants."

He could tell by the way her mouth turned down that she wasn't talking about the way the elephants got to eat so many apples.

After two more apples she shoved her hands into her pockets. "I should go."

"Are you sure? I mean, I wanted to show you the giraffes. Remember?"

"I can't." She hung her head for a moment then took a deep breath. "If my father finds out I'm feeding elephants at the zoo—" She scooted toward the door. "No telling what he might do."

"Wait," Whit called as the door banged shut. Behind him Tony shouted. "Whit, you know better than that! You trying to start a stampede?"

Whit threw down a carrot. The Bird Girl was gone. "I don't know what I'm trying to do." It had all happened so fast. Stella was there, and then she wasn't. He didn't know if he should run after her, or if he should just let her go. If only he knew the rules for dealing with friends.

Tears pricked his eyes. He was confused, and it made him mad to be confused. He suddenly felt unsure of everything and he couldn't remember why he'd ever wanted to talk to Stella in the first place.

He kicked the door frame as he exited the building. It hurt his feelings that she just walked out like that. As if they hadn't spent the whole morning talking and getting to know each other.

Whit forced himself to stop and think about it the way a scientist would, with some distance. He pulled out the digital recorder and pressed the button. "Subject spooked. Cause unknown." The last thing Stella said to him was something about her father. How he'd be mad if he knew.

Of course! He slumped against the wall of the

Elephant House. Her leaving probably wasn't about him at all. It had to do with her father. How she was scared of his reaction.

He scanned the crowd. He had to find Stella and tell her he understood. She couldn't have gone far, not in the few minutes that had passed. If he hurried, he could catch her before she made it to the front gate. Then he could say the words he hadn't been able to think of in the moment.

The sun heated Whit's face as he sidestepped a line of preschoolers, all of them decked in Zoo Camp T-shirts and paper nametags hanging from colored string. He nodded to Hannah, a camp counselor who'd watched after him a few times when his parents attended those big fundraising galas where they auctioned off painted ostrich eggs.

"And there's Ferdinand!" Hannah said in her bright voice as the peacock waddled from behind the restrooms and spread wide his feathers. Good old Ferdinand, always eager to please. The only time Whit had ever seen him get nasty was once when a guest smuggled in a tiny Chihuahua in a handbag and Ferdinand started screeching like an old lady whose purse had been stolen. One of the guests heard the screams and dialed 9-1-1 to report some sort of attack at the zoo.

It was such a good story that when the paramedics discovered that the screaming woman was actually a territorial peacock, they contacted Channel 6. It must have been a slow news day because reporters came right out with their cameras and the story aired that night. For weeks afterward, all sorts of guests came in asking for Ferdinand. Yep, at the zoo even a peacock gets his fifteen minutes of fame.

Whit pulled his eyes away from Ferdinand and scanned the sidewalk for Stella's white T-shirt and dark cascade of hair. The crowd was thick now, so he had to weave his way past strollers and groups congregating around the ice-cream cart. He checked his watch as he moved. 11:35. No wonder it was busy. It was the high-traffic time between the end of the 11:00 a.m. sea lion show and the beginning of the 12:00 p.m. river otter show. Vivian said they sold more ice cream in that hour than any other time of the day.

Whit picked up the pace until he was at a jog. He didn't want to wait any longer to tell her that he under-stood, that he wasn't mad or anything, he just wanted her to be okay. He needed to do it now, while the adrenaline was pumping through his body. Otherwise, the words would never get said.

When he finally spotted her, she was zipping through the crowd like a bird of paradise doing a mating dance. "Wait," Whit called, though there was no way for her to hear him. He had to get her attention before she walked out of the zoo. Otherwise his chance would be lost. Because he'd promised Ms. Connie he wouldn't leave the zoo again. He'd promised he'd honor the Number Three Rule.

He waved his arms. "Stella!"

When she turned, Whit could see her eyes were moist, as if she'd been crying. Part of him wanted to comfort her, to tell her everything would be okay. But it was too late. She was already past the first row of cars in the parking lot.

"Please," Whit said, his hand gripping the iron post. Which wasn't at all what he'd meant to say. "Stay just a little longer." Desperation made his voice higher pitched than usual.

She shook her head. "Whit, I can't."

He wished he was two years old again and could just throw himself to the ground and kick and cry.

She looked at the pavement then back at him.

"But—" she took two steps toward him. "You could come with me." Her voice was solid, confident. "To my house. Come find out why I've got to run away."

Whit nearly stopped breathing. How many times had he imagined a friend inviting him over? He pulled his hand away from the gate. Stella was asking him to go with her. And not just to the Picnic Pavilion. She was asking him to go completely away from the zoo. Across the road and into *her* world.

The way he saw it, he had no choice. It was an opportunity he couldn't possibly pass up. That world was out there waiting. And here was a friend willing to show it to him.

7 ✳ STELLA'S HOUSE

They walked along the zoo driveway, past the Zoo Lodge where Whit lived with his parents, past the picnic tables that swarmed with kids, past the flag that flapped "Meadowbrook Zoo." When they got to the main road, Stella looked both ways until it was clear, then dashed across and waited for Whit on the other side.

The cars sounded like small cyclones as they whipped past, and all Whit's senses kicked into high gear. He wondered if it had been like this for Neesha, the aging cheetah, when she'd escaped last year. It wasn't like fight or flight at all—it was a sensation of being held in place like a lightning rod, the body attracting all sorts of currents. No wonder Neesha didn't run and instead crouched low in the ditch, making it easy for her keepers to send a tranquilizer dart right into her hip.

Whit glanced back at the zoo. How long before someone came after him? There was no time to waste. He waited for a red pickup truck to pass, then sprinted across the pavement.

Stella grinned. "You're fast." She motioned toward the tall chain-link fence that marked the edge of the Botanical Gardens. "But can you crawl?"

Of course he could crawl. "This is the way to your house? Through the gardens?"

"Mama says it's safer than the road."

Sweat dripped down the side of Whit's face. Sneaking out was hard work in this kind of heat. He didn't know what to think as Stella shrugged out of her backpack and dropped to her hands and knees. As she shimmied under the fence, dragging her pack behind her, he wasn't at all sure he would fit. He was taller than she was, and thicker. How embarrassing would it be if he got stuck? He could just imagine that scene: his mother shouting orders as one of the zoo employees used a shovel to dig him out. Or worse, someone else tugging at his legs, yanking him free.

He shook the thought away and sucked in his stomach. If ever there was a time to just go for it, it was now. Stella was waiting.

As he worked his way under the fence, he couldn't imagine why the Botanical Gardens had a fence in the first place. It wasn't like the maple trees were going to make a dangerous escape. And he didn't think anyone would want to steal a plant, even an exotic one like an orchid or the night-blooming cereus he and Ms. Connie had come over at midnight to watch bloom the year before as part of his plant cell biology lesson.

They walked along the narrow path through the fern glade. The tall pines offered relief from the brutal sun, but probably due to the drought, the ferns were brown and brittle looking. They didn't look like a lush prehistoric forest the way they usually did.

Whit had been here a few times with his parents. It's where they took him when he complained, "All we ever do is stay at the zoo." Vivian would draw up her brow, and it was like he could almost see into her brain, how she was pushing all the drawers closed that held the zoo stuff. She'd shake her head and say, "How 'bout a picnic at the Botanical Gardens?" And off they'd go, the three of them. But after a few minutes those drawers in his mother's head would pop open again, and she and Tony would start talking about how Joey the kangaroo was acting lethargically, or the mysterious bald patches on the back of a fruit bat. And Whit would feel just as forgotten as ever.

But today was different. Today he was with Stella.

"Are you sure this is okay? With your parents I mean," Whit said as they walked past the Bog Garden, where flytraps waved and a dozen varieties of moss carpeted the ground. He wondered how her parents would feel about the surprise visit.

Stella pointed at the tall green domed building ahead. "Don't you love the greenhouse?"

"Not this time of year." Much as he loved the banana trees, it was an oven in there during the summer months.

Stella agreed that winter was the best season to visit. "We're almost to my house."

Whit's shoes sank into the pine straw that carpeted the forest floor, making him think of quicksand. He didn't want to tell Stella that he'd never been past the greenhouse. He didn't want her to know that it scared him a little, not knowing what to expect. He'd never been inside an apartment. But it was nothing to freak out over. Better just to trust her. The Bird Girl seemed to know just what she was doing.

Finally, through the trees Whit could see a long

brick building with green trash cans in a row. Which meant they must be nearing the end of the gardens. But there was no fence in sight. It made sense when you considered the fact that the gardens were supposed to be all natural and everything. And on this side there was no busy road to consider. There wasn't even a path in this part of the garden, just giant pines and leggy dogwoods. And patches of poison ivy everywhere. It made Whit itch just thinking about it.

He remembered the time they'd cleared the property for the Savannah Point exhibit, how he'd been playing just outside the roped-off area when the workers set fire to a pile of brush. Two hours hadn't passed before Whit began to itch as if he'd been bitten by a hundred ants. His mother said the poison ivy must have drifted by way of smoke. She reached for a bottle of Benadryl, but before she measured it out, she got to worrying about the animals getting poison ivy, too. She grabbed her walkie-talkie and broadcasted an urgent Code Yellow. And forgot all about the Benadryl. Whit had to measure it out himself.

"We're here," Stella said. Now that they were closer, Whit could see more than just brick and trash cans. The window screens were busted out, and the gutters were bent and rusted. Someone had strung a wire from a window to an oak tree, and it currently held a floral bed sheet and two brown towels. One of the trash cans was overflowing with Miller Lite beer cans, and there was a small beagle-like dog chained to a grill. The dog strained against the chain as Stella and Whit approached, wagging its tail furiously.

Stella gave it a pat on the head. "Hey, Poppy."

Whit bent down to pet him, too. "Is he yours?"

"I wish." She scratched Poppy under the chin. "He belongs to our neighbor Juan Carlos. His dad says dogs can teach kids responsibility. But *my* dad says a dog is too much trouble."

Whit rolled his eyes. A domesticated dog wasn't any trouble at all. "You want trouble? Try a bush dog. Now that's an animal that'll make you crazy. They're wound tight as a spring. Not like this little guy at all."

"Querida?" A tiny dark-haired woman with dark circles under her eyes poked her head out of the second screened door. "Who are you talking to?"

"Hey, Mama." Stella then said some words in Spanish that Whit didn't all the way understand. He knew the word *querida* from all the Spanish-speaking tourists that came with their children to the zoo. Ms.

Connie told him it meant "dear" or "sweetheart." Something like that.

Stella switched to English. "Don't worry, Mama. It's just my friend Whit." The stream of Spanish that followed was so fast that Whit couldn't even begin to interpret, even after Ms. Connie's diligent efforts to try and teach him. Languages clearly weren't his thing.

Wow. It had never occurred to Whit that Stella might be Hispanic. Until now she hadn't uttered a word in any language other than English. And that tiny tornado-talking woman was her mother. He nudged Stella with his elbow. "So this is where you live?"

"This is it." She curled her fingers into a fist and stared at the building, her face blank and unreadable. When she turned, her eyes weren't dancing the way they had at the zoo. "Are you sure you're ready?"

Whit swallowed. She was scaring him a little, but he didn't want it to show. He plastered a smile on his face and resumed his earlier role as Billy the Kid. "After you, little lady."

This time her smile was so brief he wasn't entirely sure it had happened. His heart pounded as he followed her inside.

8 ❧ THE NEXT ROOM

It took Whit's eyes a moment to adjust to the darkness of the house after the brightness of the sun, but he knew right away he was in the kitchen because it smelled of eggs and bacon.

Eggs and bacon drowning in cigarette smoke.

The odor was so intense, Whit fought the impulse to cover his nose. He breathed through his mouth instead—a trick he'd picked up at the zoo.

The first thing he noticed after the smell was Stella's mother at the sink rinsing off the breakfast dishes. Her smile was tentative, and she wouldn't meet Whit's eyes for more than a second. She ran the cloth over the same dish again and again, never once stopping to turn off the faucet. As water poured into the sink, Whit had to resist the urge to remind her of the drought. His mother would have a fit if she saw so much water wasted.

The entire kitchen was different than what he was used to. The floor was covered in linoleum that was peeling in places. The walls were a dingy yellow-gray, and one of the cabinets above the refrigerator was missing a door. Whit could see a box of store-brand Cheerios on the top shelf and two cans of tomato soup on the bottom. It wasn't anything like the rainbow of cereals on the shelf at Whit's house. Or the carousel of soup.

Whit followed Stella into the living room where a TV blared. It was the Weather Channel reporting heavy rain on the West Coast. The light flickered across the paneled walls, and Whit wished someone would lift the blinds to let some natural light into the room. As it was, he could just make out the shape of a man in a tattered recliner. He was wearing a white T-shirt just like Stella's. Only his stretched across his big belly.

"What do you want?" His voice was hard, like one of the seals at feeding time. A smoker's voice, rough and raspy, but also edged with something else Whit couldn't quite put his finger on.

Before Stella had a chance to answer, her mother

moved into the doorway, water dripping down her arm from the plate she held in her hand. "Phil, it's just Stella. She's got a friend over. Isn't that nice?" She spoke to him as if he was a small child.

Phil leaned forward in his chair, making the springs groan. He was most definitely *not* a small child. "I told you not to bother me when I'm watching the Weather Channel." The barking was so abrasive Whit fought the urge to cover his ears. "What's wrong with you?" he continued to rant. "Girl, can't you hear?"

"Go on, now," Stella's mother said to them as Phil continued to bellow. His voice thundered as they scurried past him. Whit was sure it could be heard way back at the Japanese gardens.

"See?" Stella said once they got down a narrow hallway and into the last room on the right. She closed the door behind them, but it did little to muffle the sound of Phil's shouting.

"Is he like that all the time?"

She sighed. "Some days, like today, he just yells. But other days—" She shook her head. "We're just lucky he's had his pain pills today."

Whit swallowed. He wasn't ready to ask what happened on a bad day. So he stuck to the most concrete thing he could think of. "What does he need pain pills for?"

Stella sat on the edge of her bed. Her room was perfectly neat, the bed made up with crisp corners. The spread was a dull blue color that probably had been bright blue to begin with. "He used to drive trucks. You know those big eighteen wheelers?"

Whit nodded his head. Those big trucks came in once a week with monkey chow and horsemeat and assorted fruits and vegetables for feeding the animals.

She paused to tuck a strand of hair behind her ears. "He was in a wreck. His truck skidded on a slick bridge and the trailer flipped into a ditch."

"Wow. When did it happen?"

Stella looked at her hands. "Six years ago."

Whit's eyes widened. The way they acted, he had expected her to say it happened six *months* ago.

"When I was five," Stella said. "He broke his back and had three surgeries, but they told him he can never drive a truck again. So he just sits in his chair smoking cigarettes and popping pills." She drummed her fingers on the bedspread and looked at him hard before she continued. As if she was daring him to look away.

When he didn't, she let out a long sigh. "Except on the days he forgets to pop the pills. Or runs out of them."

His throat tightened. He wasn't sure he wanted to know what came next. "Wow. That's awful." Even as he said the words he knew how inadequate they were. He scrambled to change the subject. "Hey, you didn't tell me you could speak Spanish. Where are you from?"

"Here, silly." She rolled her eyes. "I was born here. But my parents—my father met my mom when he went to truck-driving school in California. He and his driving buddies were always skipping over the border, just for fun. And to do laundry."

"Laundry? Really?"

She nodded. "It's cheaper there. So that's where they met. At a Laundromat. My mom says it was love at first sight."

Whit didn't know what to say. The two people he had just met didn't look anything like "love at first sight." And he should know, because that's what his parents always said about when they first met. It happened when his mother did an internship at the Meadowbrook Zoo during veterinary school. Tony helped her file Millie's toenails, and that was it. They got married eight months later. Now it seemed like they were hardly ever in the same room together, but when they were, they were always holding hands or something.

He looked around the room. "Weird. I figured the place would be plastered in drawing of flamingos."

She pressed her lips together. "Yeah, well. You know where the TV is, in the other room?" When he nodded, she continued, "My father used to hang all my drawings up there with little thumbtacks. He liked my pictures so much he'd pull them out from under me before they were even done. And they were stupid, you know? Just stick people and blobby sunshines." She shook her head. "I don't think he even remembers that I draw. Nobody does. Well, except Mama. And Hugo."

And now Whit. A little thrill rushed through him. He loved that she'd chosen to confide in him, that she let him in on her secret passion. But she still hadn't answered his question. "But you could put them up in here, right?"

She looked at her hands. "One day when he wouldn't stop yelling, I just started ripping them all down to get his attention. I thought it would get him to stop."

"Did it work?"

When Stella shook her head, Whit wished he hadn't asked. "I just wadded them all up," she continued. "Threw them in the trash can."

Whit got an image of all that artwork trapped in a black bag, then set out in the metal cans for a truck to take away. "What about your new ones?" She'd nearly filled her sketchbook. "You could put those on the wall."

"Maybe." She bit her lip as she looked around the room. "I can't believe I just told you all that." She met his eyes and held them for a long moment. "You're so—" She tossed a stuffed bear at him. "Calm."

Warmth spread through Whit's body as he clutched the bear. Stella liked him. She liked him so much that she trusted him with her secrets. He wanted to give her the same warmth, so he confessed a secret of his own. "Ms. Connie says I'm sort of like a duck. Calm on the surface but paddling like crazy under the water."

She waggled her hands like a duck's feet. "You make a good duck then. I never knew all that was going on underneath."

"Did you know I picked you?" He swallowed. "For my field study." He pulled the recorder from his pocket. "That's how interesting you are."

"No way." She cocked her head. "Really?"

"Yep." He rewound and played all the parts he'd recorded so far.

"So I'm like a science project." She giggled. "Cool."

As they continued to talk, Whit reconsidered the room, the house, everything. Phil was still yelling, but now it felt more like hiding out in the basement when a hurricane was blowing over. The walls shook, but they also absorbed some of the sound. And it seemed to help that they couldn't see what was going on in the other room.

"Whit, promise me you won't tell anyone about my father, the way he is. Hugo says I can't tell people or it will ruin our whole plan." She rubbed her temples. "To change things for good. He says I've messed it up enough already."

"Why would he say that? What did you do?" The words were out before Whit could control them.

She blew out a big breath. "I just kept hoping, you know? I thought if we just gave him enough time, he'd get better. And things could get back to the way they used to be. Before the accident." She shook her head. "But Hugo says that's never going to happen, that the only way is to leave. But it has to be just the right time."

"You mean, like, leave for good? Not like just going to the zoo every day."

She nodded. "That's part of the plan, too. Hugo told Mama to get the family pass, to get me out of the house. But my father doesn't know anything about it. He'd be mad if he knew."

"Because of the money?"

Stella gave Whit a quick look then lowered her eyes. "Because he thinks zoos are unnatural. That it's cruel to keep animals in cages."

Phil had stopped yelling and the room was silent. Whit thought about the man he had just seen in the recliner. What did a man who sits all day in front of the Weather Channel all drugged up know about the zoo?

He'd heard it before, the argument against animals in captivity. The animal rights people were all about returning animals to the wild. But they hardly ever had a plan for learning about the animals. And they cared even less about conservation. It was because of zoos that species like black-footed ferrets and Spix macaws and plains bison had been saved from extinction.

And that was just the big picture. The truth was that zoo people cared deeply about animals. Whit's mother spent every waking moment fretting over the animals' welfare. And probably at this very moment Tony was washing out gallons of elephant diarrhea. There was nothing cruel about it.

He sat beside Stella, but didn't look at her. He was shy again, suddenly aware of where he was: at a friend's house. In her bedroom. He needed to know they were on the same side, that Stella bringing him here hadn't been some big trick. "But *you* like the zoo, right?" It was the closest he could come to asking if she liked *him*.

Stella didn't hesitate. "Well, yeah. It's better than being stuck here." She picked at some snags on the bedspread. "Hugo says . . ." She pressed her lips together as if deciding how much to tell him. "Hugo says it's not safe for me here. That my father might do the same thing to me as he did to him."

Whit didn't want to ask, but he had to. "What do you mean? What did your father do?"

She covered her face with her hands and started to cry. "It's bad. Really bad."

Her tears only added to the tightness in Whit's shoulders. "It's okay. You can tell me."

"One day he ran out of pills, and the doctor said it was too soon for more." She wiped her tears and her voice got stony. "Hugo said something about how if the doctor was smart, he'd quit giving pills to him at all, and my father—" She swallowed. "Mama says he didn't know what he was doing. But he had a gun in his lap. We didn't even know he had a gun! He couldn't even lift it all the way, he was so jittery. But before any of us could do anything, he pulled the trigger." She shuddered. "The bullet hit Hugo in the leg."

When Whit's mouth dropped open, she looked away. He couldn't believe her father had shot Hugo. His own son. "Come on. You're kidding, right?" He stuttered as he struggled to find words. "W-w-were you here when it happened? Is Hugo okay?"

She nodded and pulled a frame from her dresser. It was a photograph of a boy who looked so much like Stella that Whit knew it had to be Hugo.

"I saw the whole thing," she said. "But Mama said we couldn't tell the police. Because they might take us away. She told me she'd buy the zoo membership if I would just tell the police I hadn't seen a thing." A tear slipped down her cheek. "And that's when Hugo left. He said he couldn't stay here in this house. He had to leave."

Whit's heart thudded with such force he couldn't

help placing a hand on his chest to feel it. It was like something you'd hear on one of those stupid afternoon talk shows. Only it had happened to Stella. And right here—just a short walk from the zoo.

He pressed against his chest and made himself take a deep breath. He couldn't believe her mother would tell her to lie to the police. Between the two parents, no wonder Hugo ran away.

But Stella's mother was so sweet. He swallowed, remembering how just the day before he had been completely happy when Ms. Connie said she would lie for him. It *was* easier than the truth sometimes.

He forced his thoughts in another direction. "So if all that hadn't happened—" Whit couldn't bring himself to say the more specific words. "Then you never would have come to the zoo. We never would have met."

Her eyes brightened. "Mama would say '*no hay mal que por bien no venga.*' It means 'good always comes from bad.' You know, like a silver lining."

He grinned. No one had ever called him a silver lining before. Until another thought crossed his mind. "Does he still have the gun?"

She nodded. "He keeps it under his chair."

Whit stood up. The room seemed to close in on him as he pictured the gun. All Phil had to do was reach down and grab it.

He paced in front of the bed, fighting the urge to flee. He didn't feel safe, but he didn't want to leave Stella.

She grabbed his arm. "So now you know. And that's why you can't complain about your parents. Because what you have is so much better than this."

Whit stared at her.

What she said was true.

And it wasn't.

Yes, it was an awful situation. Clearly Stella's family needed help. But that didn't make Whit's problems any less important. Stella telling him that he couldn't complain was like saying you can't complain when you have a sore throat because there are people in the world who have cancer.

Oh, he could complain all right. Stella didn't have the corner of the market on unhappiness. It was just different, that's all. Their situations were completely different.

"Stella, you get out of here every day. You draw birds. You do what you want." He looked from one bare wall to the next. "I'm stuck in the zoo every single day. I don't have any real friends. My parents would rather care for a Komodo dragon than me." Whit ran his hands through his hair. "And that's a reptile, you know? It's not like you can cozy up with them." He took a breath. "I mean, patrol and attack. That's all they do. But my parents find it fascinating."

Stella smiled. "Well Komodos are pretty cool. If you like dinosaurs."

Whit did a double take. She wasn't mocking him—she was teasing him. He laughed and shook his head. How did she do that? He'd never met anyone before who could say just the right thing to yank him out of his anger and make him feel instantly lighter. He eased back onto the bed.

They sat wordless for a moment. Whit wondered what was going on in the rest of the apartment. It was quiet now, but Stella's parents were still there doing something.

Parents. Whit heaved a sigh. Had his noticed yet that he was gone? He wiped a smudge off the face of his watch. 2:57 p.m.

"I should go," he said. "The day's nearly gone."

"Can you find your way back?"

Whit visualized the route they'd taken. The worst part would be going back down the hallway past Phil. "It's not that hard."

Stella cracked open the door and peeked down the hall. "Phil's napping. If we're quick, he'll never notice."

Whit followed Stella. The Weather Channel still blared, but Phil had pushed his chair into a reclining position and a slight snore rattled each time he breathed in. Stella stood in front of him and stuck out her tongue. From the small table beside the chair she grabbed a black lighter and stuffed it in her pocket. She left behind the large plastic cup, remote control and a half-empty pack of cigarettes.

As they entered the kitchen, a hiss of steam rose from the iron in Stella's mother's hand. She had set up an ironing board between the stove and sink and was ironing a pair of blue jeans. She kept her voice low and spoke in rapid Spanish. Whit wondered if she did that because she didn't want him to understand what she said. Or maybe it was just easier for her than English.

When Stella responded in the same fashion, Whit figured it was probably just the way they talked to each other all the time. Maybe they didn't even realize they were doing it. He tuned out the words and concentrated on the action. He had never seen—nor heard of—anyone ironing blue jeans. His parents hardly ironed anything at all. Only occasionally, when his mother had an important meeting. It's not like the animals cared what they looked like.

Finally the conversation slowed and Stella pulled open the screen door. "I'll be right back, Mama."

"*Si, querida.*" She waved her hands to shoo them out of the room. "*Vete, por favor.* Quiet now while he is sleeping."

Stella nodded and held the door open while Whit scooted through. He hardly even noticed the heat as he pulled in several breaths through his nose. After all that smoke, fresh air never smelled so good.

Stella eased the door closed and stood on the top step. "I hope Millie starts feeling better."

"I wish you were coming."

"Mama needs me. For when he wakes up."

Whit crossed his arms against his chest. Hugo had probably told her when Phil was sleeping wasn't "the right time" for her to leave her mother. And maybe he was right. But it didn't stop the disappointment from making his shoulders slump. It all sounded so foreign to him—as if Hugo and Stella were the grown ups and their parents were the children. Whatever complaints he had about his own parents, they were always the grown-ups.

"But —" He didn't want to leave her. And he didn't want Phil to wake up. Ever.

"Here." She dug inside her front pocket. "Take this." She tossed him the lighter.

Her aim wasn't all that great, so he had to really reach to catch it. The lighter was heavier than he thought it would be. "What am I supposed to do with it?"

"Keep it," she said, and ducked back inside the door.

As the latch turned and the bolt slid into place, Whit turned it over in his hand, then held it to the light. It was imprinted with the name Zippo.

"Rhymes with *hippo*," he said aloud, and was sorry Stella hadn't heard his joke.

As he turned to go, the little dog Poppy whined. Whit knelt beside him. "It's okay, little fella." The words were as much for himself as for the dog. He was so uncertain now, like maybe he knew too much, had seen too much. It would take him a little time to process all the information.

He glanced back at the closed door. He'd have to

ask Ms. Connie for a refresher course in Spanish. And maybe request a research project about the gun laws. And addiction to pain pills.

He gave Poppy one last stroke, then threaded his way through the gardens and leaped across the road. At the zoo entrance he dashed behind a large jogging stroller and slipped right back inside the gate.

Each time Whit broke a rule, it got easier.

9 ❦ BIG SNAKE DAY

The next day Whit had no lessons with Ms. Connie. It was the second Saturday in June, which meant it was the zoo's annual Big Snake Day. Basically it was just a glorified medical exam for the snakes. Instead of recording all the measurements and weights inside the Reptile House, Doc performed the duty on stage at the center arena while the guests watched.

The most popular snake in the Meadowbrook Zoo's collection was Pete the reticulated python. Zoo staff always asked for volunteers to help hold Pete so that keepers could perform the checkup. And the guests loved it. People were fascinated by the snakes, but scared, too. It was like a train wreck—they couldn't look away.

Snakes didn't bother Whit. He wasn't particularly fascinated, either. The most interesting thing they did was eat. But most of them were fed only once a week. The keeper would put a frozen mouse inside the enclosure, and Whit would watch for a few minutes as the bulge moved down the length of the snake's body. And that was that. The rest of the time the snakes pretty much spent coiled and sleeping.

His eyes widened as he looked out from the front gates. There wouldn't be any coiling and sleeping for Whit today. Not with the size of the crowd. Whit didn't know where they had all come from. One thing was for sure—the drought hadn't stopped anyone from coming out for the event. The line was so long for entry at the front gate that one of the summer volunteers had rolled the ice-cream cart into the parking lot to offer refreshments to people as they waited to get their tickets.

As the "Welcome" banner flapped above him, Whit's attention drifted away from the snakes. His mind flashed up scenes of Stella. Her fingers moving the pencil in sure, confident strokes. The sparkle in her eyes when he told her his dad was head elephant keeper. The way she bit her lip.

Then darker images. The crumbling apartment building. Stella's tiny little mother leaning out the door. The overpowering smell of the house. The sound of

Phil barking his orders from his sad lump of chair and belly and blanket in front of the TV. Stella snatching the lighter from the table.

Whit fingered the lighter in his pocket. Felt its smooth weight. Not only had he talked to Stella, he'd been inside her house, met her parents, hung out in her stark bedroom. She'd given him a souvenir.

As he shielded his eyes to better see her if she came gliding across the parking lot, he pictured the bare walls of her bedroom. There was something missing, something more than the absence of art on the walls. It was like the empty, eerie feeling that hollowed out his stomach when he watched one of the big cats, a Siberian tiger maybe, pace a worn trail just inside the glass of the enclosure.

They'd had one like that once at the Meadowbrook Zoo. Her name was Siretha. Back and forth, back and forth she'd go. Whit's mother said it was a sure sign of unhappiness. That's when his mother sent in the enrichment experts, when an animal was doing repetitive, mind-numbing things.

For Siretha a crew of zoology students created a fake zebra out of cardboard. They painted it and everything. Then Doc stuffed it with bits of meat, and the keepers positioned it in the enclosure. Sure enough, as soon as Siretha was released from the sleeping area, she dropped low into the grass and stalked the zebra. It didn't take her long to shred it, but the experience was enough to interrupt her habits, to challenge her mind.

Was Phil the tiger? Or Stella?

He shuddered and pulled out his digital recorder. "Big Snake Day. Subject absent. Or better hidden than a Mariana fruit dove." The Mariana fruit dove was a shy and secretive bird that avoided detection by roosting high in the forest canopy. What he would give to see Stella cut through the crowd.

Whit gave up his vigil when Ollie Tucker approached in his brown zoo coveralls. Ollie had worked at the Meadowbrook Zoo for more than thirty years. Day in and day out, the white-whiskered man walked the zoo grounds with a toothpick practically glued to his bottom lip. He'd chew on the toothpick as he swept up popcorn kernels and half-eaten hotdogs. Whit cringed at the thought of still being stuck at the zoo after so many years. Especially when he was sure guests would still litter, no matter how many trash cans they put up. The worst was the soggy ice-cream cones. Once the sun had its way with them, Ollie had to scrape those up with a hoe.

Ollie waved Whit over. "Whit! Your mother just put out a Code White. Said you're late. She needs your help loading the snakes right away."

Whit sighed. "Thanks, Ollie. I'm on my way."

The Code White was probably the highlight of Ollie's day. Maybe even his week. No way was Whit ever going to sign up for a humdrum job like Ollie's. And just thinking about his mother made him clench his fists. As long as Whit was there when she needed him, she didn't care a bit about how he spent his Saturdays. Sometimes it seemed like he only existed when she happened to think of a job for him to do. A job, which she would refer to not as a job, but as part of his *education*.

The walkways were crowded as Whit made his way to the Reptile House, where the keepers had the venomous snakes in a red hot box for safe travel across the zoo grounds. Hot boxes were kept locked, and they had a special lid with a double door—one solid and one screened. And only keepers were allowed to handle them, no one else.

For the smaller snakes, the Level I nonvenomous snakes like the garter snake and the rat snake and the corn snake, such precautions weren't necessary. They were bagged in pillowcases that had been turned inside out, so that the snakes wouldn't get their scales damaged by any rough seams. Then the pillowcases were placed inside small Igloo coolers that even a guest could carry. As the keepers loaded the hot boxes, Whit held one cooler in each hand. It was his job to deliver them to the team of volunteers that waited in the arena.

The small set of bleachers was completely filled, and the area in front of the stage was thick with guests. Hannah was in charge of entertaining the crowd while they waited for the measuring to begin. Whit listened as she asked for volunteers with snake jokes to take the stage. Some of them were really funny. Others didn't draw a laugh at all.

Finally there was only one person left on stage. Whit groaned when he recognized the man as one of the regulars. He always told the same joke.

The speakers screeched as Hannah placed the microphone in his hands. "Why did the two boa constrictors get married?"

Whit mouthed the answer as it was announced.

"Because they had a crush on each other." The crowd tittered as expected, but it bothered Whit just a little bit because the joke wasn't true. Boas, like pythons, didn't crush, they constricted. They simply squeezed their prey enough to cut off their air supply. Bones didn't break or even crack. Certainly there was no crushing.

Not that the average guest would even care about accuracy. The jokes were just time killers anyhow. He wondered what Stella would think about the joke. Did she even like snakes? He shook his head. There was so much more he wanted to know about her.

The keepers started with the smallest snakes first, so Whit set the coolers down and cracked them open. One by one the staff volunteers removed the snakes, measured them, then walked through the crowd where guests were invited to touch, if they dared. A second volunteer followed with a huge bottle of hand sanitizer. The last thing Whit's mother needed was some guest getting salmonella and plastering the story all over the news.

Whit scuffed his shoe in the dirt. He wished he'd remembered today was the day of the show so that he could have told Stella about it. Then they could have watched it together. He might even have gotten the keepers to pick Stella when it came time to measure Pete. If it's something she would have liked.

Pete had lived at the Meadowbrook Zoo for twelve years. He must have eaten hundreds of thawed rats and rabbits to get so big. The keepers stretched him out, and the crowd cheered as Whit's mother got busy with the tape measure. "Thirty-one feet long," she announced with a smile. Her face glowed with excitement, and Whit got an image in his mind of Stella's mother with her worried eyes. Did she ever glow? He wondered if she did anything besides wash dishes and iron and placate Phil. As much as it annoyed him sometimes, he thought it was probably better to have a mother that was busy doing something she was passionate about. Ms. Connie said that was one of her personal goals for his schooling: for Whit to find the thing that *he* was passionate about.

Well, he could tell her with certainty that it wasn't snakes. Or telling jokes that weren't even based in fact. He was still trying to figure it all out.

By the next morning any remnants of Big Snake Day had been stowed away for the next year. The zoo lot was empty by comparison—but still pretty full for a Sunday. This time Whit didn't wait at the zoo gate.

And he didn't hide in the shadows of the Reptile House either. He sat on the bench where Stella usually sat, checking his watch every few minutes. He'd hardly been able to sleep the night before, and he was achy and full of questions. He couldn't wait for Stella to get there so they could go explore some more of the zoo. He wanted to show her everything. So that at least for a while she could forget about Phil and Hugo and everything that made her so unhappy at home.

Today he would take her to the Predator House where the keepers were getting ready to introduce the Siberian tiger cubs to their permanent enclosure. There were two of them, a male and a female. Their mother was named Ranee, which meant "Queen." Ranee had lived at the Meadowbrook Zoo for seven years and had given birth to them after breeding through the Species Survival Plan (S.S.P.), which was the system zoos used to choose the healthiest mating pairs. It involved examining bloodlines and medical records. Whit couldn't even estimate the number of hours his mother had spent looking over different animals' S.S.P.s.

The cubs were something to see. They were constantly in motion, always jumping, chasing and chewing—nothing like the danger they would eventually be. All the keepers had to do now to interact with them was wear thick gloves to protect from those sharp teeth and strong jaws. Not like later, when a tranquilizer gun was required, and each keeper would carry a can of pepper spray. Just in case. And Whit's mother required them to keep a fire extinguisher, too. Not for fire, but to stun an unruly tiger. Whit had seen it work with his own two eyes.

It was hard for Whit to believe that just a few months ago those two active cubs had been helpless and blind. And now they had outgrown the nursery and were ready to meet the guests.

It was always a mystery how the animals would react to their new home. Whit's mother said change was difficult for all animals, but especially for ones in captivity who were not accustomed to much variation in their daily lives. Whit thought Stella might enjoy watching the cubs explore their new territory. And he would be careful not to say anything about Phil or Hugo or his feelings about his own parents. His goal was to be a good friend, one that could help her forget all her troubles.

From the other side of the zoo, the little steam locomotive whistled.

Oh, good. The train was up and running. It had been shut down for two days the previous week due to an engine problem. Now that it was fixed Whit's mother would be pleased—it meant more money generated in ticket sales and fewer complaints to field. The train was one of the best things about the zoo. It took you all around the perimeter of the property, behind the elephant house and through a little tunnel. It was a great way to cool off on a blazing hot day like this one.

Sweat dripped down the side of Whit's face. He wondered if Stella had ever ridden the train. Maybe that's what they could do today, after the Predator House. Whit grinned as he considered sharing the zoo with her; suddenly it was an exciting place. Even the uncomfortable memories of her house couldn't kill his mood.

The train whistle tooted as the first load of passengers departed from the depot. Whit checked his watch again. Yep, the train was right on time. But still no Stella.

10 ✱ RODNEY'S QUESTION

Whit ambled up the walkway toward the turtles. Only one was sunning itself today, probably on account of the unbearable heat. Whit fingered the back of his neck. It was hot to the touch. He'd have to stop in at the first-aid station and get some sunscreen.

He sat on the wall and watched Stella's bench. As much as he hated to record depressing data for his field study, he knew it needed to be done. "Subject nowhere in sight," he whispered into his digital recorder. "Bench remains empty." Ms. Connie would be pleased by his scientific accuracy.

As he reached for a pebble to toss into the water, he heard his father's voice. "Whit! You've *got* to stop throwing rocks into the turtle pond. It sets a bad example for the guests."

Whit closed his fingers around the pebble but held it close to his leg. What was Dad upset about? Usually it was his mother who said things about how he had to be aware of the example he set. Not his father.

And it wasn't just that. Tony's face looked haggard, too. Whit remembered the pools of diarrhea in the Elephant House and wondered if his father had gotten any sleep at all the night before. His irritation probably had nothing at all to do with the pebbles or the guests or even Whit. "How's Millie?"

"Completely dehydrated." Tony shook his head. "I can't figure it out. Doc can't, either. We're just trying to keep her standing."

Whit pushed himself up from the wall of the turtle pond. This wasn't good news. "Did Doc start an IV?"

Tony nodded. "At about midnight. I just hope we didn't wait too long to get it going." Tony clenched his fists. "I should have called Doc sooner. But I thought it would pass. I thought it was just all those banana stems we fed her."

Whit really didn't want to talk about the elephants. It's not like there was anything he could do to help anyhow. "Well, I'm sure you're anxious to get back to her. You *are* her favorite keeper."

A smile softened the circles under Tony's eyes. "She's come to love Jerry and Helen, but Millie's still my girl." He reached out and tousled Whit's hair. "Come by later, okay? Maybe by then we'll have some good news."

His father's rubber boots slapped against the concrete as he walked away. Whit let out a long breath. Sometimes there were benefits to his parents' single-mindedness about the animals. All he had to do was talk the zoo talk to distract them from any concerns they might have about him.

He let the pebble drop into the turtle pond with a solid plunk. If he waited for Stella another minute, he thought he'd go crazy.

As he turned toward the Reptile House, a group of kids walked past—three guys and three girls. The guys all wore baseball caps and T-shirts with "Meadowbrook Football" emblazoned on the front. The girls had their hair fixed and their faces made up, and they were constantly leaning into one another to whisper and giggle. The only one in the group that noticed Whit was a short, dark-haired guy who was working a yo-yo. He met Whit's eyes and nodded, as if to say, hey, I see you over there.

Whit nodded back, careful to imitate the nod precisely. As the group moved on, he watched the yo-yo sliding up and down and wondered what it was like to be one of them—to be so pleased with one's own world that nothing else mattered.

He didn't want to be that way. Not really. The world was too amazing to ignore. But he envied the way they seemed so at ease. And how they were so clearly a group. Just like the chimps in the Primate House. There might be a pecking order, but whatever it was, each one *belonged*.

He picked up a discarded zoo map from the sidewalk. As he unfolded it, his insides felt heavy, like they were sinking down around his ankles and making it impossible to move. Wherever it was that *he* belonged was not pictured.

As a white-haired couple dressed in Sunday clothes came along and claimed Stella's bench, Whit followed Ferdinand as he waddled up the walk. Without any warning whatsoever Ferdinand stopped and spread his feathers. All that shimmery brilliance was enough to lift Whit's spirits.

"You're the best, Ferdinand," he said as he dashed under the wisteria-covered arbor that marked the entrance to the Predator House. Might as well go ahead and see those tiger cubs.

Whit entered through the front door, then punched in the code that allowed him to access the first runway, which was a narrow, concrete hallway that led to a special safety cage. All the big cat enclosures had this extra security area and a whole list of additional rules due to the danger involved in working with them. Whit usually wasn't even allowed to enter the safety cage, even though it only led to a second larger runway. It was too risky.

His mother waited with the cubs inside the second runway, along with a news crew. Whit straightened his shirt and smoothed his hair as one of the keepers escorted him through the safety cage. Vivian's smile was electric under the bright lights. Of course. This was exactly the kind of coverage his mother craved. New babies at the zoo were the best kind of advertisement. And it worked, too. When baby Lila first went on display zoo attendance shot up twenty percent. Yep, the guests loved the babies. And they would love these little ones, too.

Whit knew better than to interrupt the camera crew, but he did wave so that Vivian knew he was there. She waved back. "Whit! Come on over. Rodney wants to ask you a question."

Rodney Carmichael was the reporter who did all the zoo news. Whit had seen him lots of times. He had gray hair, but he used words like *cool* and *awesome*, and he always gave Whit a high five.

Whit ran his fingers along the steel bars. Last time Rodney had asked him what was his favorite animal at the zoo. Now *there* was a loaded question. It was only after Whit had answered with his standard, "giraffes" that his mother informed him it would be better if he had mentioned the sea lions, since they had just started a new act. And if there had been any sort of bad press, like an animal escape, then Whit would want to avoid mentioning those animals. It was a way more complicated question than it sounded. Better just to avoid the situation. "No thanks. Not today."

"Come on, little man. I just want to get you on camera for half a minute," Rodney said.

Vivian gave him a hard look. "Whit, please. Don't you want to be on TV?"

Whit knew it wasn't a request. And now that she had schooled him, maybe he wouldn't mess it all up.

Whit nodded, and as his mother came over to let

him into the enclosure, the camera crew adjusted themselves to include Whit in the picture.

Vivian touched him on the shoulder. "Be yourself, Whit." She leaned close and whispered so that only Whit could hear. "Just don't mention Millie's illness."

Heat colored Whit's cheeks. As if he would be so stupid as to mention the elephants. Did she think he didn't listen to her at all? He fought the urge to cut and run as Rodney took his spot and the camera crew ran a sound check.

Two seconds later it was too late. "And we're rolling."

The bright lights made Rodney's blue eyes appear bigger. "We're here at the Meadowbrook Zoo talking with Dr. Vivian Whitaker about the Siberian tiger cubs. Just joining us is Whit, Dr. Whitaker's son and lifelong resident of the zoo."

The camera panned to Whit, and as the lights hit his face, Whit had to restrain himself from shielding his eyes. "So, Whit, what's the best part about living at the zoo?"

"The best?" Whit chewed his lip and thought of Stella. Was there a best?

He glanced at his mother. Her eyes were bright and

expectant. He had to say something. Something good. Something that would make people want to come to the zoo.

Whit swallowed. This is the part he'd played his whole life so far. Little zoo boy. Dutiful son. But he didn't choose this life; his parents did. And he was tired of it. He wanted to be one of those kids wearing the Meadowbrook football shirts. He wanted to come with a group of friends. He wanted to come with Stella.

Stella, who hadn't shown up today. And who knew when she would ever come?

He couldn't keep this up—this life of watching and waiting. He needed to go after what he wanted. And that started with his mother. He had to stop just going along. He had to do something to make her pay attention not just to the Red List of Endangered Animals and the S.S.P., but to him, Whit, her son.

He took a deep breath. Then, when his voice came, it was loud and clear. "Rodney, the truth is, I hate the zoo. My parents are the ones who love it. Not me. Every day when I wake up, I wish I was someplace else."

11 ✳ A NICE BOY

When the news came on that night, Whit was still in his room, where he had been banished as soon as the TV crew left the zoo. It didn't matter that Rodney had promised his mother not to run the piece that included Whit. Vivian was still furious. And embarrassed. Whit knew that was the part that hurt her the most.

Whit could hear them through the thin walls. "Don't worry about Whit," Tony said, his voice defeated. "He's just having a bad day. And he knows how serious things are looking for Millie."

Whit wadded a piece of paper and threw it at the wall. Were other people's fathers like this? Tony just couldn't fathom Whit having any emotions that didn't revolve around what *he* cared about, which was, of course, the elephants. Sure, he was sorry to hear Millie wasn't improving. He hated seeing Tony so distraught. But you'd think that his father—and mother, too— would realize he had other more important things to worry about.

His mind flashed to Ms. Connie. She'd be disappointed, too. But she knew there was more to him than animals. She was the only one who treated him like a regular kid. Like the other day when she'd caught him outside the zoo gate. She was upset, but she also seemed to understand why he was there. She was the only one who seemed to hear him when he said things about wanting to go to regular school, about wanting to be around kids his own age.

Tony's voice came again. "Closing the Elephant House was the right thing to do. I know it means lots of complaints from the guests." There was a pause, and Whit imagined his mother's face set in a scowl. This was the part where Vivian would keep quiet, and Tony would smooth things over. "I'm doing the best I can, Vivian," Tony continued. "It's awful down there. Especially now that Wanda and Lila have started with the same symptoms. I've got to get back as soon as I can to relieve Jerry. And we may need to bring in some extra help. We can hardly get one mess cleaned up before one of them starts up with the diarrhea all over again."

"Thank goodness the press didn't get hold of the news about the elephants today," Vivian said. "The public needs these happy, healthy cubs! Attendance has been down all month. I think it's the drought that's got everyone on edge." There was a pause, then Vivian's voice came back softer. "Even Whit."

Whit leaned his head against the wall and looked up at the ceiling. The glitter stars he'd glued up there so many years ago still sparkled. Back then fake constellations were enough to satisfy him, and the Meadowbrook Zoo never seemed small.

What would Stella think of his room? He wondered if the fact that she'd invited him to her house meant that he should now invite her to his. It seemed like there was some rule about reciprocation. And he wanted her to come over. He wanted to show her some walls that weren't bare. Heck, his walls weren't even clean. Chores around the house had never been a top priority for his parents. Not with all the animals right there within walking distance.

Whit fiddled with his digital recorder, checking to be sure there was plenty of battery power left. He pressed the button and began to make an update for his field study.

Only there was nothing to tell. He hadn't seen his subject all day. He pressed the playback button instead; to be sure he'd included everything. And that's when a thumping sound come from the other room, as if something had fallen to the floor. Then he heard his mother scream.

"Whit! You get in here this instant."

Whit leaped to his feet. What in the world? As soon as he pulled open the door, he knew. His father's chair was empty, and Vivian was standing in front of the TV. On the screen right next to his mother and the cubs was Whit telling the whole world how much he hated life at the zoo.

His throat tightened and for a second he couldn't get a breath. "But Rodney said he wasn't going to run it!"

Vivian's eyes were small and hard. "Well, he did, didn't he?" She clenched her jaw then slammed down the remote, making the screen go black. "Whit, do you realize what you've just done? Everything is ruined now."

Whit had no answer. All he knew was that he was on TV and his mother's head was about to explode.

Most of the time she barely even saw him, but now her eyes were heat-seeking missiles. She didn't even look up when the phone in the kitchen began to ring. It was like she was frozen in place, with shoots of smoke streaming out of her ears. And Whit was frozen, too.

When Vivian's cell phone also began to ring, Whit knew just what was happening. Members of the board had seen the news. Now they were calling to talk about damage control, same as they did anytime something bad happened.

Whit took one step back, then another. It was just like that time one of the crab-eating macaques had bitten a keeper's finger clean off. The news broadcasted the story, and right away the calls came pouring in. Everyone wanted to talk to Vivian to find out how such a thing could have happened.

He had to get away from her. He had to escape. Before things got any worse than they already were. He backed away from the TV without saying a word. Then as she reached to answer the ringing phone, Whit crept out the front door, careful not to let it slam.

The night air was thick and turning darker by the minute. The sun had already dropped below the tree line. Whit raced down the lighted path toward the zoo parking lot. It was all but empty now with just a few of the employees' cars left. Whit eyed the big barn where the one dairy cow and a pair of Yorkshire pigs slept in mounds of soft hay. He could wait there for things to settle down.

Or, he could go someplace else. Someplace entirely different.

He walked to the edge of the parking lot and looked down the long driveway. Stella's house was just across the road and through the gardens. He'd only been there once, but he knew he could find it again. It was just a matter of putting one foot in front of the other.

Yep, that's what he'd do. He'd go to Stella's. He'd knock on her door and say, "May I please speak to Stella?" as if he visited her every single day. He'd ask her why she hadn't come to the zoo today. And he'd tell her about what happened with Rodney. He'd tell her everything. And she would listen in that way of hers, with the same undivided attention she gave the birds as she penciled in every last detail. Stella would hear him, and she would understand.

As the night frogs trilled, Whit watched for headlights on the street. When none appeared, he dashed across, his breath coming in quick spurts. But he did it.

And he realized he was getting used to his life as a renegade. If only the dark wasn't closing in so quickly.

He shivered and hurried through the gardens, careful to place each of his feet on firm ground. The last thing he needed was to trip and fall when not a soul in the world knew where he was. It wasn't until he saw the shape of her building that he allowed himself to take a couple of deep, noisy breaths.

Whit didn't have any idea what Stella would think when she saw him. And unlike before, when he had planned and practiced for days what to say to her, this time he didn't have a script. He just knew he had to see her. She was the only one who might possibly understand. She was the only one who might possibly *listen*.

Poppy the little dog pulled against his chain as Whit approached the door to Stella's home. A light shined through the kitchen window, and even from outside Whit could hear the Weather Channel. Whit imagined Stella's mother at the stove cooking supper, Phil in his chair, and Stella in her plain little room. The last thing they would be expecting was Whit at the door.

Whit gave Poppy a pat then knocked on the door.

He listened hard, but there was no sound of feet, no voices, nothing but the TV.

His hands shook. Probably he didn't knock hard enough.

"Stella!" he said as he knocked a second time. "It's Whit." He scolded himself for not knowing Stella's mother's name. First *or* last. Stella had never said, and Whit hadn't thought to ask.

Stella's mother's face appeared as she pulled the curtain back to look out the window. Whit waved then held his breath as she pushed open the screen door.

Her brow crinkled and she looked back over her shoulder. Back toward Phil. "Hola." She stood in the doorway and pulled the door close to her. "You want Stella?"

"Yes. I mean, *si*." It embarrassed him a little but that exchange was pretty much the best he could do. "I just—" He shoved his hand in his pocket where the lighter rested snug against his leg. "I just want to talk to her."

She shifted her body away until only her head stuck out of the opening. "Phil . . . Mr. Taylor . . . he won't like it." She bit her lip. "But Stella says you are a nice boy. So I will get her for you."

Whit couldn't stop the grin from spreading across

his face. A nice boy. Stella said he was a nice boy! And now he knew her last name.

"*Gracias*, Mrs. Taylor. *Gracias*."

While he waited for Stella, Whit bounced on the balls of his feet. He couldn't keep still. All the anger, all his discontent about the TV interview and his parents never paying enough attention just disappeared. He was in the world that existed outside the zoo. And soon there would be a friend to join him.

12 ❧ THE CAROUSEL

Stella slipped out the door as silent as an owl swooping in for a mouse. Her dark hair was pulled back from her face, held in a pink rubber band.

Whit grinned. He was so happy to see her. "I was just wondering," he started. He couldn't believe what he was about to suggest, because it meant going right back to the place he'd just left. But the zoo was the only place Whit knew. And he had a hunch Stella would like his idea. "Want to come ride the carousel with me? It's really cool at night. And no waiting in line."

"The carousel? No way!" Which by now Whit knew meant "way." Her voice sounded excited and impressed, same as it had when Whit told her about his parents working at the zoo.

"Sure. But you can't tell anybody, okay? I'd get in big trouble."

She grinned. "I thought you were already in trouble. In fact, I figure that's why you came in the first place. Because you need a place to hide out."

Whit lifted his eyebrows. So she'd seen him on TV. She knew what happened.

Stella leaned down so Poppy could lick her face. "Bet that didn't go over so well with your parents."

Whit was glad for the darkness because he could feel his cheeks get warm. "Yep, my mom is pretty mad. But hey, how did you see it? I thought all Phil watched was the Weather Channel."

"He likes Channel 6, too."

Whit heaved a sigh. Everyone liked Channel 6. "How bad was it?"

Stella giggled. "You left Rodney speechless. That's pretty amazing all by itself."

"Well, he deserved it. Ask a stupid question . . ."

Stella finished it for him. "Get a stupid answer."

Nearby some cicadas started up, filling the silence. Whit swung his arms the way he did sometimes when he was nervous. He didn't know what else to say. It was like he had used up all his wit and cleverness for one conversation and now his mind was a black hole.

Inside Phil's voice burst through the walls. "I'm sick of tacos. Can't you ever cook anything else?" A pan clattered to the floor. Stella's mother let loose a stream of Spanish that Whit didn't understand.

Stella linked her arm through his. This close, she smelled like cigarette smoke. "Let's go. I want to ride that carousel."

Whit followed her along for a couple of steps, then stopped. "Your mom. Will she be okay?"

"She'll be fine. He had his pills today. So she'll make him a hamburger and it'll be fine."

Whit listened hard, but didn't hear any more shouting. He didn't want to leave Mrs. Taylor if it wasn't safe. At the zoo all the employees were trained to bypass zoo security and call 9-1-1 if there was any sort of violence. His mother was a big proponent of the "better safe than sorry" approach. "But what about the gun? Does he still have it?"

Stella nodded. "Under his chair. And one of these days I'm going to steal it."

"Really? What would you do with it?"

"Hugo wants it. Getting the gun is part of our plan. But Hugo says it has to happen at just the right time. Otherwise it could just make things even worse."

Whit was silent as he worked to make sense of this information. For a kid who ran away, Hugo sure was involved. Whit always thought that if you ran away it was forever. Like you could never come back. But it sure didn't seem to be that way between Hugo and Stella. It sounded like they talked pretty often, and Stella did just what he said. But what if Hugo's plan was wrong?

Before Whit could ask Stella about it, the sound of her parents' voices rose again. The shouting felt so urgent. It made him want to shrink behind a trash can.

Stella pulled on his arm. "Come on. It's fine. It happens nearly every night."

Every night? Whit closed his eyes. It wasn't normal. The feeling he got in the pit of his stomach when he remembered walking through Stella's house wasn't normal. It just wasn't.

But then the doubt started creeping in. How was Whit supposed to know what was normal? Living your whole life at the zoo didn't leave much room for learning about normal. Unless you counted knowing what was a normal amount of elephant poop. Or what was the normal activity level of a ten-foot alligator.

Whit looked back at the window where the kitchen light shined. The easiest thing would be to trust

Stella. It was her house, so she should know, right? Besides, he really wanted to take Stella to the carousel. He wanted to spend as much time with her as possible.

When Stella tugged on his arm a third time, Whit followed. As the sky faded to black, they picked their way through the gardens and across the road until they were once again in the zoo parking lot. It was at this point that Whit took the lead. "This way," he said, swinging to the left, away from the Lodge where Vivian was probably still fielding phone calls.

As they passed the front gate, Whit remembered the bulging crowd on Big Snake Day. The emptiness was almost eerie at night. As if there were no animals, no enclosures, no zoo rules. At least until one of the sea lions barked or the monkeys screeched.

At the side door to the Education Building, Whit keyed in the code and pulled open the door. It was as dark inside as it was out, but Whit didn't want to risk revealing their location by turning on any lights. His mother, if she happened to be looking, might even see it from the front door of the Lodge. "Just follow the wall with your hands," he told Stella. "This hallway leads straight to another door that opens near the children's playground." He pictured the spiderweb-shaped rope obstacle course and musical water fountains. "From there it's only about fifty feet to the carousel."

They ran their fingers along the textured wall across closed doors and bulletin boards that held push-pins and slips of paper, both large and small. From the back of the building they heard a rustling sound, then "Nut Nut. Nut Nut."

Whit froze. Of course. They might hide from his mother, but there was no hiding from Nut Nut, the blue hyacinth macaw that lived in a cage at the back of the building. Whit knew the curator of education always covered Nut Nut's cage with a sheet before closing up for the night, but that didn't mean she couldn't hear. "Nut Nut," the bird said again, this time louder. "Nut Nut. Nut Nut."

Stella grabbed the top of Whit's arm.

"Don't worry," he reassured her. "It's just a macaw."

Her grip loosened, but she didn't let go.

"Haven't you ever met Nut Nut?" Whit said. "She's one of the animals that the Education Department takes out for school visits. She's so friendly, and the kids like her bright feathers. You'd have to go to Brazil to see one in real life."

"Can she talk?"

"She's supposed to. Macaw's are known for their vocabularies. But Nut Nut—that's all she ever says. 'Nut Nut.'"

"Maybe you could teach her. I bet she'd learn if someone just took the time."

Whit sighed. That's what he'd thought too. Until he tried it. "My independent study project in fourth grade was to teach Nut Nut to talk. I spent hours talking to that bird. I even burned CDs and left them playing at night. But it didn't work."

"I know about things not working." She paused. "I used to pray for my dad to get better. I'd kneel beside my bed, just like Mama taught me. I promised to do all the chores without being asked and to keep my grades up and everything." She shook her head. "He still woke up yelling at my mom and me. And Hugo, before he ran away."

Whit wasn't sure how they'd gotten from his fourth grade project to Hugo, but he liked it. He liked that their conversations went deeper than small talk. "I know what you mean. Some things I guess just aren't going to change no matter what."

"Hugo says we have to *make* things change. Like he did, when he left. That's why we have a plan. When the time is right, I'm going to fly away too."

Whit could feel the air close in around them. The cool boys on TV didn't have conversations like this. They always said something funny or changed the subject. "Well, I haven't given up on Nut Nut." Whit swallowed. "I just moved on to other projects. Like, have you ever seen the Madagascar hissing cockroaches? Ever wondered what makes them hiss?"

"Cockroaches that hiss? Really?"

Relief swept over Whit as he told her all about the cockroaches, how they're unlike other insects because they make that hissing sound by exhaling through their breathing holes. He even did an imitation of their defensive sound, which made Stella laugh. When his hand finally landed on the doorknob, he twisted it and they hurried out into the night air.

The big barn loomed to the right and the carousel was straight ahead. Whit tipped his imaginary hat. "Your ride awaits, little lady."

Stella giggled again and ran toward the carousel. "I get the swan."

"Then I'll take the lion." Usually he liked the giraffe, but it was on the opposite side of the swan. It really didn't matter to Whit so long as they were close enough to talk to each other.

The metal poles that held the hand-carved animals were cool to the touch. Whit wished for more light so he could show Stella the amazing detail painted on each animal. He remembered carousel shopping with his mother, how she wanted to get the most accurate animals possible. Whit didn't know if it mattered to the average guest, if they even noticed the details. But showing it to Stella like this, it made him proud that it was a real work of art, not some cheap ride at a traveling amusement park.

While Whit fiddled with the control box to put the carousel in "silent" mode, Stella found the swan and climbed aboard.

The carousel jolted to a start. The swan and lion glided up and down as the carousel made its slow turns, and Whit welcomed the cool air on his forehead and neck. It had been such a long day. But now here he was, with Stella.

A feeling of peace settled over Whit. Like at this moment, he was exactly where he was supposed to be. It was almost enough to make him forget about the TV madness and Stella's situation.

Almost, but not quite.

13 ❋ JOE DIMAGGIO

Whit and Stella talked for hours. Eventually they dismounted the animals and lay side by side on their backs as the carousel spun them through the darkness. It was almost like being on some other planet entirely. Every now and then Whit got the urge to look at his watch, but he pushed that thought away. What difference did it make anyway? However late it was, he just wanted the night to last and last.

When his eyes got heavy, he rubbed them hard and tried to think of something else to talk about. He didn't want to go to sleep. "Want to hear some animal escape stories?"

"You mean that really happens? I thought that was just on TV."

It happened all right. More often than the average

person knew. He liked being the one to give her inside information. "Most zoos don't like to keep a record of escapes. But it's fairly common. This one zoo in California had thirteen escapes in one year."

Her voice was screechy with surprise. "That many?"

"Most of the time it's due to human error. Like when a keeper forgets to latch a gate. Or goes into an enclosure alone. My mother hates when that happens. It makes the whole zoo look bad."

And that's when the conversation switched from animals to parents. "My mother hates for things to look bad, too," Stella said. "She gets really embarrassed about my father. When the neighbors stop by, she hardly ever invites them in. She doesn't even go to her Bible study anymore. When I asked her why not, she said it's our business, not theirs. That she doesn't like the way they look at her. Like they are sorry for her."

"I don't get it," Whit said, although he *did* understand how much easier it was to just keep quiet about the bad stuff. "It's not her fault Phil acts the way he does. Probably her friends just want to help." At least that's the way Whit felt about Stella. He wanted so much to help. But he didn't have any idea what he could possibly do.

When Stella's voice came again, it was soft and mumbly. He could tell she was getting tired, too. "Mama's just—I don't know. She's scared. If Phil didn't have that stupid gun she wouldn't worry so much. Everything would be better."

The next morning Whit was startled out of sleep by a familiar voice screaming, "Help! Help! Help!" He jerked up, banging his head on the carousel pole that held the tiger. Beside him Stella rubbed the sleep out of her eyes. Staring at them from the concrete was Ferdinand, his feathers in a half spread. Even after all these years the peacock's cry still had the power to send Whit's heart rate off the chart. It sounded so much like someone in trouble.

Whit turned his watch around on his wrist, until the face was visible. 5:23 a.m. "Stella! We've been out here all night!"

Stella sat up, her eyes still squinty with sleep. "Are you sure?"

Whit jumped up. "Yep. It's morning all right." He couldn't keep the panic from his voice. The sky was getting lighter by the moment.

He tensed. They were going to be in so much

trouble for staying on the carousel all night. As fun as it had been the night before, now it seemed like a complete disaster. Much worse than the other day when he left the zoo property.

What would their parents say? He could only imagine how Stella's parents might react. The way Mrs. Taylor worried over Phil when he was right there in his house, he was sure the woman would be wiping down the counters and scrubbing the baseboards with a vengeance. When she got done with the blue jeans, who knew what she'd start ironing next. The family's underwear? He pushed away an image of Phil in his chair, T-shirt starched instead of wrinkled.

Whit paced in front of the carousel. "What are we going to do?" He was pretty clear about what his own parents' reaction would be. Vivian would bellow and charge. When she ran out of words she'd promise him a "serious talk," which would never happen because some other disaster would inevitably come along to grab her attention. As for Tony, he would launch into a story from his boyhood. Whit would pretend to listen, and Tony would pretend to understand.

He shook his head, mad at himself for being so careless. Especially on a night when there was already so much concern about the condition of the elephants, not to mention the TV broadcast. This could only make things worse.

Stella touched his arm. "Just don't say we should go back home, okay? I'm not ready. And it's not like Mama would call the police or anything. That's the last thing she'd want."

Police? Heck, Whit hadn't even thought of that. He searched the sky and half expected a sudden swarm of helicopters to appear overhead.

Stella casually twisted her hair into a ponytail. The rubber band snapped into place. "Besides, my mom was the one who said I could go with you. And unless my father asks her directly, which he won't, she's not going to volunteer that information." She kicked at the dirt and her shoe was consumed by a cloud of dust. "She says that sometimes it's best to just leave out some of the details. She says it's her way of protecting him. And us."

Whit's eyes widened. "But what if Phil somehow found out? What would he do?"

"It's not like he's going to get out of his chair and start looking for me." Her voice broke a little as she said it. He could tell it still made her sad to think of her father the way he was, and not like he had been before. Back when he displayed all her art on the walls. "My mom would probably say I was sleeping over at Juan Carlos's house." She tucked her hair behind her ears. "Sometimes I *do* sleep over there. They have five kids, so one more never seems to matter. It just makes the Monopoly games last longer."

Whit liked the thought of long Monopoly games with a bunch of other kids. "Juan Carlos?" He didn't have a face for him, but he did remember the name from when Stella had introduced him to the little dog chained to the grill. "Isn't he the one who takes care of Poppy?"

"Yeah. He just lives two doors down. He's only a few months older than me, but he'll be in seventh grade when school starts back, not sixth."

"Meadowbrook Middle?"

When Stella nodded, Whit sighed. It seemed like everybody went to that school. He reached out his hand to Stella. "We've got to go back."

She tucked her hands under her thighs, refusing his offer. "But I don't want to."

"Come on," he said, reaching again.

Stella turned her head. She wasn't budging.

Whit could feel sweat popping out on his nose. The longer they were gone the worse it would be. Even Ms. Connie wouldn't be able to save them.

Ms. Connie. Anytime Whit started to dig his heels in the way Stella was doing right then, Ms. Connie would back off a little. And sure enough, Whit would abandon his argument.

He decided it was worth a try with Stella. He touched her arm. "How 'bout I tell you one more story. A really good one. Then we've got to go, okay?"

Her smile was all Whit needed to know he'd won. He launched into an escape story. "You know Neesha, our cheetah?" When Stella nodded, Whit continued. "Well, she was in heat. You know, when they want to mate? Usually the keepers track these things, but Neesha's so old, no one knew it was even possible. Until Neesha found a way out of the enclosure. I remember some kid came running up to Ollie and told him there was a cheetah on the sidewalk near the bathrooms. Ollie knew if he made any sudden movements, the guests would freak out. So he casually put down his broom and dustpan and called a Joe DiMaggio."

Stella wrinkled her brow. "A Joe DiMaggio?"

"It's code for 'animal escape.' Of course if a guest heard that on one of the keeper's walkie-talkies, there might be panic in the zoo."

She nodded, affirming the wisdom of the code. "So what happened next?"

"Doc arrived at the bathroom in question with a dart gun in hand. But they didn't even need it. As soon as Neesha saw her keeper holding out some pieces of raw chicken, she followed her like a puppy back into the enclosure."

"So that was it? Neesha didn't get punished or anything?"

Whit shook his head. "Nope. She just had to stay in her bedroom until the keepers could investigate how she escaped."

"I don't know what I'd do if I saw a cheetah loose. Probably just watch."

"Then you'd be just fine. Because Neesha's not really a threat. Unless you're smaller than she is and you all of a sudden start running. Then her hunting instincts might kick in."

"So as long as I don't run away from you right now, you won't attack?"

Whit curled his fingers like claws and made a

growling sound. "As long as you come back later, everything will be just fine."

She giggled then, and Whit's heart lightened. Everything would be okay. For both of them. It had to be.

Whit walked with Stella back the way they'd come. Inside the Education Building Nut Nut started up before he'd even gotten the code punched in. Whit checked his watch again. Thankfully the Education staff didn't start as early as the rest of the zoo employees, who were probably half-way through the morning feedings by now. Taking the short-cut through the building would allow them to get away without as much chance of getting caught.

"Poor Nut Nut," Whit said. He imagined her in the darkness of her sheet-covered cage, hearing everything but not being able to see it was just Whit and Stella passing through, not her keeper coming with an early breakfast. "Between this and last night's unexpected visit, she must be so confused." They'd certainly disrupted her routine.

Stella didn't reply, just kept heading down the hallway to the door that opened into the zoo parking lot. She didn't need Whit to lead her this time, and it was like she was on autopilot. She held her arms closer to her body, and her shoulders were hunched tight. That easy way she had of walking was completely gone now, and he realized that even though she was still on zoo property, her mind was ahead of her body—probably imagining what things would be like when she got home.

Whit followed her through the door and tried to keep up as she jogged across the parking lot. Now that she'd decided to go, she wasn't wasting a minute. "Bye, Bird Girl," he called, as they reached the sidewalk that led to the Lodge. But either Stella didn't hear him or she chose not to respond.

As her body got smaller and smaller, Whit's stomach twisted in knots. He had the awful feeling that he might never see her again. That this might be the last image he ever had of her. He wanted to shout, "Stella, wait!" But he couldn't. Not if he wanted to slip back into his bedroom without being noticed.

Whit tiptoed up the path to his house, his feet hardly making a sound. At the back door, he slowly twisted the knob. Yes! It was still unlocked. He came into the kitchen and gently pushed the door closed.

When he turned around, he froze. Vivian was sitting at the kitchen table, still in her bathrobe, her hands hugging a mug of coffee.

14 ❋ ABOUT MILLIE

"So you heard," his mother said. "About Millie."

Whit's heart pounded. He had expected her to launch into an inquisition. Instead she was talking about Millie.

Vivian looked at him from over the rim of her coffee. That's when he noticed her eyes were red and swollen. Either she'd been crying or hadn't slept. "We're all heartbroken, Whit. It always hurts when we lose an animal we've come to love." She set down her cup and reached her hand toward his. "But you know we'll get through this. It's going to be tough, but it just comes with the territory."

Whit's head was light and he was afraid he might fall if he didn't grab on to something fast. He steadied himself by gripping the back of the chair next to his mother as his brain strained to keep up.

He had been so worried about his parents' reaction to his night out on the carousel. He should be relieved. Instead anger made the tips of his ears red. It didn't matter what was going on in Whit's life. Zoo business always came first.

He wanted to throw her coffee cup against the wall. He wanted to hear the ceramic shatter. Until what his mother was saying about Millie sank in. *It always hurts when we lose an animal.*

What she was telling him was not that Millie was worse. It wasn't about diarrhea anymore. His mother was telling him that Millie was *dead*.

Whit swallowed. His father was probably in pieces right now. Millie had been his girl for so long. "What about Wanda and Lila?"

Vivian lifted herself from the chair and set the cup in the sink. "I don't know. They're both younger, so that helps. All we can do is wait and see."

Something like gratitude washed over Whit, although he couldn't tell if it was for himself or for his father. He just knew one dead elephant was tragedy enough. But to lose all of them? It would be beyond devastating.

"I've got a news conference scheduled for nine

o'clock this morning." She folded her arms and leaned her backside against the countertop. "Leave it to Millie to give a gift even in death. The public will be so consumed by grief they'll forget all about your little stunt yesterday with Rodney."

Whit's face flushed. He hated the way she was talking about Millie's death as if it was a good thing for zoo business. It made his shoulders tense. "It wasn't a stunt."

"Oh, Whit." She touched his cheek with the tips of her fingers then jerked them away. "Don't you realize I hate it sometimes, too? Do you think I *enjoy* mornings like this?"

Whit shoved the chair into the table, causing the salt and pepper shakers to fall. She came so close sometimes to acting the way he thought a mother should. But then she detoured and it was once again all about her. Not about him or Tony or even Millie. It was about the zoo.

Whit stalked out of the room. If she had been an animal in the zoo collection, they would have proclaimed her an inadequate mother. Like the time Koko the gorilla wouldn't nurse her infant at all, just kept sweeping him across the floor of the enclosure. Keepers tried for days to model the appropriate behavior, but she'd have none of it. The infant was a plaything she had no idea what to do with. So they placed him with a surrogate instead.

Whit slammed the door to his bedroom and threw himself onto the bed. She didn't even know he had been gone. All night! He squeezed his eyes against the hurt. Even Phil with his painkillers and cigarettes would notice Stella's absence. How drastic an act would it take to hold her attention?

He sighed. His father, he could sort of understand. He had been distraught about Millie. He wouldn't have had time to notice Whit's empty bed.

He rolled over and stared at the stars on his ceiling. So many animals at the zoo had died over the years. It was just the way things worked when you were dealing with exotic animals—and one of the main reasons Whit thought they made terrible friends. You just couldn't count on them to stick around. There were so many mysteries, so many things scientists still didn't know. If there was anything good to say about it, it was that that's how they learned what was best for the animals—through illness, death, and other failures.

Whit lifted himself to sitting, then pulled out his digital recorder. "Millie dead. Mother same as ever. Subject's reaction unknown." What a worthless update. His summer field study might go down as the most ridiculous one ever.

He sighed and pushed off the bed with his hands. He knew what he needed to do, and there was no point in putting it off any longer.

When he left the house this time, he let the door slam behind him. Let her wonder where I'm going, he thought. She thinks she's so smart—let her figure it out.

Instead of making his way through the Education Building, Whit walked right through the front gate, then along the nearly empty walkways to the Elephant House.

He swallowed hard before he keyed the door for entry. Whatever waited on the other side of the door, Whit needed to be strong.

The smell assaulted him as he let the door close behind him. It was worse than it had been the day he'd brought Stella. Even mouth breathing didn't all the way work and Whit had to fight the urge to vomit.

Millie was sprawled on the ground in her enclo- sure. From his view, she looked like the bald top of a mountain. Whit watched as Tony absently stroked the edge of one of Millie's flaglike ears while the other keepers tended to Wanda and Lila.

"Hey," Whit said, his heart pounding in his ears.

Tears streamed down Tony's face. "She just wouldn't get up, Whit." He motioned to her chart, and Whit picked it up. He recognized his father's blocklike print. "June 8. Millie down at 8:30 p.m. Unable to get her to stand. Death at 4:30 a.m."

Whit set the chart down. While he was asleep on the carousel with Stella beside him, Tony had been watching an elephant die.

"Doc will be here for the necropsy in a little bit." Tony motioned to Wanda and Lila. "They've already said their goodbyes. But I've got to stay until they move the body. Just to be sure the girls don't do something crazy."

Whit sifted through all the stories his parents had told him about animal grief. At least Wanda and Lila still had each other. Surely it would help. And Wanda would naturally take the role of matriarch, because she was older.

As for the necropsy, it had to be done. It was required of all zoo animal deaths. His mother said it was

the best teaching tool ever. When scientists could figure out why something died, they could work on how to prevent death. Which Whit knew was the ultimate goal. Conservation and education. A major point of the zoo was to save species from extinction.

Whit thought of Stella. Of how he'd been able to tell her things he'd never told anyone. Things he hadn't even realized he felt and thought until the words were spewing out of his mouth. She'd only been a part of his life for a little more than a week, but he didn't know what he'd do without her. It was such a short amount of time compared to how long Tony had loved Millie.

"Dad, is there anything I can do?"

Tony put his arm around Whit's shoulders. "No, son. Just get ready for the onslaught. As soon as the news hits, we'll be bombarded with visitors. You remember how it was when Perry died?"

Whit nodded. For weeks guests had lined up outside the Primate House, their faces grim, their voices lowered to reverent whispers. He hadn't understood at the time how so many people could feel so sad about the passing of a western lowland gorilla they'd never touched, only watched through the double glass panes of the enclosure.

For the elephants there were Art Days when Millie painted for the public. And Elephant Encounters, when guests were invited to stand on a platform and pull the rope that released a bunch of produce for the animals to eat. Except the guests loved Millie way more than they loved Perry.

Whit's mind played back all sorts of scenes of Millie's daily life—the behind-the-scenes life that he had witnessed because he was the elephant keeper's son. Like when the dentist came with a jackhammer to drill out a rotten tooth. And afterward when she was so loopy coming off the anesthesia. "Too bad the guests never got to see her gobble monkey chow."

Tony chuckled. All Millie had to do was see him walk in with one of those brown bags over his shoulder, and she'd trumpet. And she'd stand still for all sorts of medical procedures so long as Tony kept the kibble coming.

Whit smiled. It was one of his earliest memories. He couldn't imagine there were too many people in the world who could say that their earliest memories included an elephant. Next time he saw Stella, he'd tell her the story. And he'd tell her this new story, too. Even though by the time he saw her again she'd probably have heard it from Phil's blaring TV.

Except, of course, the part about how Millie managed to trump Whit even in death.

He shook away the selfish thoughts. It was good that his parents hadn't known he was gone. It actually saved him a lot of trouble. Another silver lining. He wished he could remember the Spanish phrase Stella and her mother used.

"I guess I'll go then." Whit moved toward the door.

Tony nodded and lifted his hand in a wave. "Whit, wait. There *is* something you can do. Something very important."

Whit let go of the door handle and waited for his father to continue.

"Help Ollie move the bulletin boards from the Education Building to the front of the elephant enclosure. Then make a display of all the elephant art. It will be a tribute of sorts. An art tribute to a dear friend."

15 ✳ TRIBUTE

For the next hour Whit and Ollie took turns driving the golf cart to haul in the bulletin boards that would serve as makeshift walls. It took another hour just to locate all the art pieces. Whit had forgotten that there was only enough room in the Gift Shop to display four or five paintings at a time, so the rest were stashed in various storage areas around the zoo.

Once they had gathered all the supplies, they leaned against the wall for a break. He glanced at his watch. What he really wanted to do was walk over to Stella's. He wanted to find out how her parents had reacted to their all-night adventure. But the way his father's eyes had shimmered when he made the request—there was no way Whit could refuse him.

Ollie pushed against the wall they'd built. When it shifted, he shook his head. "What do you think about using a clothesline instead?" He thumped the bulletin boards. "It wouldn't be flimsy like this. And we could just string the line up and attach the paintings with wooden clips."

"You mean not use the bulletin boards at all?"

"Mmmm-hmmm."

It sounded suspiciously like starting over. "Just string it up. Simple as that."

When the older man grunted, Whit wanted to scream. After all that work they'd done to bring the bulletin boards out. And now they'd have to haul them all back.

The older man's eyes crinkled as he poked at his teeth with the toothpick. He didn't seem a bit bothered.

Whit looked again at his watch. He figured the more decades a person spent at the zoo probably the less time mattered. He thought about asking Ollie, but he knew the older man preferred silent cooperation. He wasn't much for making conversation. Which was just as well because Whit didn't want to hear any trash stories just then.

Might as well get it over with, Whit thought. "I'll go get the clips and clothesline from the Education

Building." He remembered Hannah using the clothesline to hang the kids' art during summer camp.

For the next two hours Whit didn't stop moving. Even after his muscles started to cramp, he still kept working right alongside Ollie. When they finished hauling back the last of the bulletin boards and had hung the final painting, Whit and Ollie treated themselves to ice-cream sandwiches from the ice-cream cart. "You're a good worker, Whit," Ollie said between licks. "Maybe you can take over for me when I retire."

Whit couldn't stop the grimace from crossing his face. The thought of being Ollie horrified him. "I don't think so." He refrained from launching into his list of complaints about living at the zoo. Ollie wouldn't understand.

Ollie grunted again, his attention turned by the small group walking away from the Elephant House, their white coats flapping against their legs. "Looks like they've finished with the necropsy."

Whit didn't say anything because he didn't need to. They both knew the departure of the vets meant that Millie's body had been moved to the crematorium. Probably the news crews were gone by now, too.

Whit wiped the sweat from his brow. It was

probably the hottest day ever, and here he was stuck in the middle of it. He could hardly breathe, the heat was so suffocating. As he walked past Savannah Point, Whit noticed that the giraffes were crowding next to the building and the zebras were gathered under a tree in the far corner. They were strangely still, except for an occasional flick of ears and tail. Whit couldn't help but wonder if they were merely channeling the mood of keepers who were quiet and methodical as they grieved the loss of Millie.

What did the animals really know? Could Wanda and Lila understand death? Could they *feel*? Whit knew there were no definite answers. And Vivian gave strict instructions to all the employees at the zoo not to enter into public discussions about animal intelligence. It was nearly impossible to measure, and people held their attachments to certain species so vehemently that the risk of offending someone was great.

As Whit walked past the ostriches, he thought no one would argue over their intelligence. And he'd never heard a guest exclaim over them the way they did the elephants and primates. The most complicated thing they did was lay really big eggs.

But then, maybe *complicated* was overrated. Whit

tucked his arms under his pits as he passed a white-haired grandmother pulling a wagon that held identical twin girls in matching purple dresses. Their enjoyment was as simple as motion: As long as the wheels turned they giggled and smiled.

He quickened his pace. He wasn't sure what would make him smile on a day like today. Seeing Stella would help. All day he'd hoped she would come sailing through the zoo to let him know everything was okay. But all day long he'd been disappointed. She was no-where. At least nowhere in the zoo.

Whit kicked a trash can, then squatted down to tie his shoe. He'd go crazy if he waited around the zoo any longer. He was nearly crazy already, and it wasn't yet noon.

He had to find out about Stella. He couldn't wait another day.

As he dodged guests on his way to the main gate, he was filled with an urgency that just wouldn't go away. He'd always felt urgent about Stella. But Millie's death seemed to make it worse. It was as if he needed reassurance of his friend's presence in the face of the loss. He needed to know she would still be there, no matter what. And it bothered him that she hadn't shown up all day. His own parents may not have noticed his absence all night long, but he couldn't be sure about Stella's. Their reaction could have gone so many ways. His throat tightened as he imagined scenario after scenario. He had to find out for himself.

By the time he got to the road, he felt positively giddy. He wasn't nervous about crossing now, just excited. And the walk through the Botanical Gardens seemed more comforting than strange. Whit liked the way the trees whispered and the clouds closed in, making the forest floor dark and peaceful.

Poppy pulled at his chain when he saw Whit, his whole body wagging along with his tail. Whit knelt and scratched him behind an ear. "Good to see you, too."

When he saw the curtains drawn over Stella's kitchen window, he swallowed hard. There was no light behind them, and not a sound coming from the house.

Whit rapped the door with his knuckles. Still nothing. He put his ear against the door, straining for the weathergirl's voice on the Weather Channel or Phil's bark or Stella's mother clanking dishes.

He knocked again, harder this time. "Stella? Mrs. Taylor? Anyone home?"

Whit stepped back as Poppy began to whine and wiggle all over. The dog's attention was focused on the dark-eyed guy coming out of the door next to Stella's house. As soon as Whit saw the yo-yo in the kid's hand, he snapped his fingers. He'd seen this guy before. "You were at the zoo. With a bunch of other kids."

The guy grinned. "Yeah, I remember you." Poppy collapsed in delight as the boy rubbed the dog's belly. "I'm Juan Carlos." He nodded toward Stella's door. "And you must be Whit."

A blush stole up Whit's cheeks. "She told you about me?"

As Juan Carlos admitted that she had not so much told him as he had overheard Stella talking to one of his sisters, Whit marveled over the fact that the one guy in the group at the zoo who'd acknowledged him was the same guy Stella told him about at the carousel.

He looked again at the closed door and dark window. Maybe Juan Carlos could help. "Do you know where they went? Stella, I mean. And her family."

Juan Carlos flicked his finger out and allowed the yo-yo to spin down the string. "Don't know. But they loaded some suitcases before they left in their car this morning. Like they'd be gone overnight."

So they weren't gone, like, to the store. More like, on vacation. Whit shook his head in confusion. "Phil can ride in a car? I thought his back was too bad for that."

"Nah. Mrs. Taylor just gives him extra pills." He made the yo-yo dance. "He was laid out in the backseat smoking a cigarette when they left."

"Where was Stella?"

"In the front, next to Mrs. Taylor. She waved to me and mouthed some words, but I couldn't tell what they were. Mrs. Taylor spun the tires as she pulled out of here. Like she was in a big hurry."

Behind them the door to Juan Carlos's opened and a stream of kids spilled out. They waved, and for a second Whit thought that Juan Carlos was going to introduce them. But he turned his back on them. "Ignore them," Juan Carlos said, his yo-yo sliding back up the string.

The rejection didn't seem to bother any of them. The tallest girl kicked a soccer ball from behind the front porch steps, and the three others scrambled after it. Juan Carlos didn't seem terribly concerned about the other kids, whom Whit assumed were his brother and sisters. Juan Carlos was so calm and cool, and he seemed to care even less about Stella and her family's earlier departure. Heck, it could be that Whit was overreacting. It was so hard to tell.

He forced his words to come out slow and steady. "Any idea when they'll come back?"

Juan Carlos let the yo-yo completely unwind until it was hanging like a pendulum from the string attached to his middle finger. "Nah. But they're never gone for more than a few days."

Whit looked at the closed door, the curtained window. He pictured the dingy kitchen and wondered if Mrs. Taylor stowed the ironing board, or if she kept it out all the time. He climbed the steps and put his ear against the door, listening for any noise.

When noise came, it wasn't from inside. Whit startled when the soccer ball clanged against a trash can, knocking the lid clean off. It rang in his ears like a gunshot.

And that's when he thought of Phil's gun. Was it there even now, lurking underneath the chair?

Whit's breath seemed to get stuck in his chest. If the gun was there and Phil was not, this was his chance to help Stella. He may not be able to change things for her, but he could at least get the gun. Stella had said herself that it would make her feel safer. And without Stella's parents home, it would be even easier than when Stella swiped the lighter from Phil's side table while he was sleeping.

Except he needed someone to act as a lookout.

His eyes fell on Juan Carlos, who continued to spin the yo-yo, completely unfazed by his siblings' rowdy game. He wished he knew the kid well enough to predict how he would react to his request.

Whit swallowed. Getting Phil's gun would also help Stella's entire family. And who knew when—or *if*—another opportunity would ever present itself?

Now was the time. "Say, Juan Carlos. Want to help me with something?"

16 ✹ THE GUN

As soon as Whit mentioned the word *gun*, Juan Carlos pocketed his yo-yo. "Seriously? You want to steal Phil's gun?"

When Whit shrugged, the other boy shook his head. "Are you sure you're the kid from the zoo? All those times I've seen you on TV, I never would have pegged you for the criminal type."

Whit lifted his chin, flattered that Juan Carlos had ever thought of him at all. "This isn't about me. It's about Stella."

Juan Carlos looked from the door to Whit and back again. "We've got to talk to my mom about this."

"Your mom?" Whit would never tell his own mother something like that. She'd think he'd lost his mind to be getting so involved in other people's affairs. And to even consider handling a firearm? She'd go ballistic.

The boy nodded. "It's no secret how things are over there. We all want something to be done."

Whit had to work to keep his mouth from dropping open. Juan Carlos was so bold and matter-of-fact. He made it sound like these were regular conversations he'd had with his mom. Like he actually trusted her. He wondered what made Juan Carlos's mother so different from his. "Okay."

As Juan Carlos disappeared into the apartment next door, Whit's whole body tingled with nervous energy. If he didn't find something to do with his hands he thought he might explode. Once up the steps, he pulled back the handle of the screen door and knocked, just to be sure. When there wasn't an answer, he slid his fingers around the knob on the regular door. It made a clicking sound and the hinges squealed as the door opened.

Whit's eyes bulged. He hadn't expected it to be unlocked. As the odor of cigarette smoke filled his nostrils, he forgot about waiting for Juan Carlos and his mother. All he could think about was getting the gun.

Whit stepped into the dark kitchen. He didn't bother turning on the lights. He knew from experience that they didn't help all that much anyway.

By the time he got to the room that held Phil's chair, Whit's head had started to spin. The TV was dark, so there was very little light in the room at all.

He crouched beside the chair and tried not to gag from the combined odor of cigarette smoke and sweat and rotting fruit. What was wrong with him? He'd always thought of himself as a pro at dealing with bad smells.

He slid his hand along the shag carpet and patted around. He ignored some paper wrappers and some bare spots where the carpet had been rubbed away. Or *burned* away. He couldn't tell in the dark. When his fingers found cold metal, his chest contracted. He jerked his fingers away, as if he'd touched a hot stove. He wiped his hands on his pants. Billy the Kid had all kinds of guns. The outlaw's favorite was a Winchester rifle that was way bigger than this one, and he sure never had any trouble picking it up. Whit shook his head and reached for the gun a second time.

This time he squeezed his eyes tight as he allowed his hands to hover in space above the gun. He visualized himself as Billy the Kid. In his mind he lifted the gun and squinted one eye as he aimed it toward a target. "Pow," he said and felt a little silly when he heard his own voice.

And that's when he heard footsteps. He blinked open his eyes and jumped away from Phil's chair.

First came a woman's panicked voice. "Where is he?"

"Whit?" Juan Carlos called. "Are you in there?"

As their footsteps came across the linoleum, Whit's heartbeat filled his ears. He'd had his chance to be a real hero and get the gun himself, but now it was gone. "In here. By Phil's chair."

Juan Carlos's mom flipped on the light switch as they raced toward Whit. "Don't get any closer. It might be loaded."

Juan Carlos stood in the kitchen doorway as his mother positioned herself between Whit and Phil's chair. Her dark eyes were shiny. "Stay back." Her voice was steely now.

Whit backed away as she reached under the chair for the gun. "Get in the kitchen, both of you," she instructed the boys. As they backed onto the linoleum, she pulled the gun into her lap and clicked open the chamber. Whit gasped as three bullets tumbled to the carpet.

He knew for sure that he was no Billy the Kid when his legs started to wobble. Three bullets.

Whit stumbled through the kitchen and followed Juan Carlos down the steps.

"Everything's okay," Juan Carlos's mother said when she joined them. She threw an arm around Whit's shoulders. "The gun's empty now." She pointed to where it lay on the steps, wrapped in a towel. "We're all safe." She patted his back and forced his eyes to meet hers. "Guns are terrible things. Do you hear me? Nothing good ever comes of them."

Whit's whole body trembled. "When the door opened, I just went inside. I just—I couldn't help it." An apology almost tumbled out of his mouth, but he pushed it back. Yes, he'd thought about picking up the gun. But he didn't actually do it. It was just so confusing. He wasn't sure anymore which rules to keep and which ones to challenge.

"No harm done," Juan Carlos said. "I knew my mom would know what to do. And now it's over. We got that gun out of there."

As Juan Carlos's mother pressed in the numbers on her cell phone to call the police to pick up the gun, Juan Carlos stroked Poppy and told the other kids

what had happened. As Whit looked at them, he felt like he was on an alien planet. He just didn't understand his own body sometimes. Why had he reacted the way he did? He shook away the memory.

He got to his feet. What he wanted was the comfort of the familiar. "I've got to go."

Juan Carlos's mother held out a hand to stop him. "Are you sure you'll be okay? Let me call someone. I don't want you going off alone."

Her concern made tears prick his eyes. She wasn't even his mother. He'd never even laid eyes on her until she came into that room. "Ms. Connie," he whispered. "Ms. Connie will come get me."

17 ❧ RAIN

When Ms. Connie arrived, she rushed to Whit. "Oh, Whit." She hugged him hard and stroked his head as he leaned against her shoulder. "What a day you've had." He melted into her.

She sat with him as he and Juan Carlos and Juan Carlos's mother, whose name was Rosa, told the whole story to the police. After the reports had been recorded, one of the officers put on plastic gloves and tucked the towel, gun, and three bullets into a plastic bag. He slipped everything into his briefcase, and the officers climbed into the patrol car.

As soon as the police were gone, Rosa said her goodbyes to Whit and Ms. Connie, and she called the children in for supper. Juan Carlos was the last to go. "It was a good idea to get the gun, Whit." He pulled the yo-yo from his pocket. "It was the right thing to do."

Whit mumbled his thanks. He was still embarrassed about rushing in without Juan Carlos and Rosa. And he was even more embarrassed about how the gun had affected him. Like he was a little child. While Juan Carlos was the picture of maturity.

"Come on, now," Ms. Connie said. "Let's get you back to the zoo."

As they turned to go, a drop of rain hit the top of Whit's ear. He looked up at the dark sky just in time to see a flash of lightning in the distance. Finally.

"Guess I should have driven over." Ms. Connie covered her head with her hands. "Hurry." The tall, old pine trees provided some cover, but Whit could hear big fat drops hitting the boughs above him. The sound was soft at first, then it got louder as the rain came harder. Thunder rumbled, and Whit instinctively ducked his head.

How many days had it been since it had rained? Since he'd met Stella, he'd lost count. He just knew it had been so long that he had forgotten the smell of it. How fresh the world seemed, how new. Like nothing bad could happen ever.

It was a lie, but he still liked it.

At the road, the smell changed. Steam rose from the hot asphalt, and Whit could smell oil and gasoline.

And even though the rain was still falling, there wasn't a puddle in sight. The ground was *that* thirsty.

Whit liked the hiss the cars made as they sliced past them, and he liked the heavy slickness of his shirt as the rain plastered the thin cotton to his back and shoulders.

Stella should be here, he thought. Ms. Connie wouldn't mind. Stella should be here sharing this rain.

By the time they got to the path to the Lodge, the thunderclouds had moved across the sky and the sun was peeking out again. Then, just as suddenly as it had started, the rain stopped.

Whit looked at his watch. "That's it? Ten minutes of rain?" It wasn't enough to make even a dent in the drought. It might as well have not even happened.

Ms. Connie pushed wet hair from her forehead as they walked across the nearly empty parking log. "Looks like the guests made their usual quick exit." Even though the Gift Shop stocked umbrellas and ponchos, guest began packing up the kids and strollers just as soon as it started to sprinkle.

Not that it mattered much at this point. The tickets had already been sold, so Vivian couldn't complain about low attendance numbers. And the shower was so short it probably didn't affect the animals in any negative way.

Whit pulled his saturated shirt away from his skin. "Ms. Connie, I think I'll stop by the Lodge and change my shirt. Meet me at the Education Building in ten minutes?" He knew Ms. Connie needed to change, too. And she liked it when he took responsibility for their lessons. And she had come so quickly to his rescue, it seemed like the least he could do.

"Whit, I can't keep this from your parents. They need to know about what happened today. The gun and the police—I've got to tell them."

He nodded. It would be better coming from Ms. Connie anyway. Plus it would give his mother time to process the information before she talked to Whit about it. He walked up the path to the front door of the Lodge. And that's when he remembered.

The art. Millie's art.

The rain had come so quickly, there wasn't any way Ollie could have gotten it covered in time. Not without help. Even if the tarps had been near the gift shop, which, Whit knew for a fact, they weren't. They kept the tarps in the storage closet of the Education Building, and that was all the way on the other side of the zoo.

Whit got an image of Tony stroking Millie's lifeless ear. He slung his soaked shirt over his shoulder and hurried toward the front gate of the zoo. He had to see what the damage was. Then he had to fix it.

The walkways were nearly empty and the air had thickened so much Whit could hardly breathe. He slowed to a walk. There was Ferdinand, his feathers tucked close to his body as he hid under Stella's empty bench.

He wrung out his shirt as he passed the Primate House and pulled it back over his head. Monkeys screeched, their voices piercing despite the heavy air. It was probably the two youngest ring-tailed lemurs, Gideon and Samson. They were always getting into a tussle. It usually wasn't serious, but after the last squabble resulted in a torn ear, Doc said they might need to be separated. They fought about everything: food, females, and who got the best resting space. It was as though they couldn't ever just be happy.

Whit wondered if that was what it was like for Stella's parents. Now that there wasn't a gun, *could* they be happy together? Could they somehow get through the pain and the pills and get back to the story Stella told about love at first sight?

For all their faults, Whit's parents were always on the same side. Sure, they slammed doors sometimes, and yelled, and once Tony had even slept at the Elephant House. But within a day or two Whit would find them again kissing in the kitchen. It was disgusting. But at least he never had to worry about a gun.

Whit jogged past where the little train sat parked under its cover, quiet and lonely. He was delaying the inevitable—he knew that. But he was pretty certain that when he got back to Millie's art tribute, it wasn't going to be a happy scene.

He sighed. Part of him wished he could be like Stella's brother Hugo and just run away and leave the problem behind. Hugo would probably concoct an elaborate plan that involved waiting and strategy and very specific timing. Whit didn't understand how Stella could trust her brother so completely when he had left them to fend for themselves.

Waiting wasn't a plan. Not really. At the zoo problems only got worse. It was best to step in just as soon as possible. And better than that was prevention.

Prevention was one of Whit's mother's soapbox topics. "If people could just *see* prevention," she said. "It they could just *imagine* how it could make the animals' lives longer and healthier, then they might donate money for larger enclosures or padded floors or subdued lighting." As it was, they were always finding out too late—after a beloved animal died or escaped or experienced a chronic illness.

When Whit finally reached the Elephant House, it was just as he expected. All of Millie's colorful brush-stroked canvases were drooping. The ones on paper were curling up in the corners, and some were already tearing from the weight of water. The paint bled and ran, making watery blobs that were no longer art at all.

Whit tugged at the clothesline. When he released it, water droplets sprinkled his face and arms as the line bounced back into place. The paintings were all ruined. Completely destroyed. Might as well throw the whole lot of them in the incinerator with Millie's body.

He yanked one large print from the line, ripping off a corner as it came loose from the clip. A growl of frustration rose in his throat as he crumpled it into a ball and tossed it onto the ground.

All that work for nothing. What a nightmare.

18 ✿ THE CALL

Whit pulled the lighter from his pocket. He didn't want Tony to see the paintings like this. He didn't want anyone to see them. It was just another thing he'd made worse instead of better. He ran his thumb across the rough edges of the little wheel. It made a clicking sound, but it didn't light.

Whit shook the lighter, then banged it against the palm of his hand. He'd seen someone do that in a movie. And sure enough, it worked. The next time he pulled his thumb across the tiny wheel, there was a flicker.

The little flame licked the edge of one of the largest, most colorful canvases, then faded. It was too wet to actually catch fire. Whit thought he remembered the day Millie painted that one, how she curled her trunk around the fat brush, dipped it in the bucket, then slopped it across the canvas, just as she'd been instructed. How

Tony had beamed beside her, as if he was the teacher and she was his star pupil.

Millie seemed to enjoy it, too. She'd work for hours. Yep, she was a regular Pablo Picasso. Whit knew Tony had always wanted to keep one of the paintings for himself, maybe hang it over the mantel. But every year someone else had come along with a higher bid, so Tony let it go. For the good of the zoo. And, he said, "because Millie can always paint me another one."

A small stream of black smoke lifted into the air. Whit let his thumb slide off the lighter wheel and massaged the spot where the textured edge had dug into his skin. Figures the lighter wasn't good for anything. It had come from Phil.

But then, Stella had come from Phil, too. Stella who had spent the whole night with him out on the carousel. Stella who had listened to him chatter on about all sorts of stupid things. Stella who was now gone.

Whit jumped when Ollie came around the corner pushing a wheelbarrow. When he saw Whit, he dropped the handles. "I know you're not doing what I think you're doing."

Whit closed his fingers around the lighter and waved the smoke away from the canvas. "I'm just—"

Ollie held up his hand. "Don't even tell me. Because then I'll have to tell your daddy and Dr. Whitaker."

Whit's heart skidded as he slid the lighter into his pocket. The last thing he needed was Ollie reporting him to his parents, especially when Ms. Connie was already doing that very thing at that very moment.

"Give me your word, Whit. No more nothing with that lighter. Not in this place. You're a better boy than that."

Whit didn't trust his voice so he just nodded. He *was* a better boy. He knew he was.

"I won't stand by and let nobody mess this place up." He chewed the toothpick. "This is my home. You're not allowed to ruin it."

Whit swallowed. Ollie only worked at the zoo, but he called it his home. Meanwhile Whit actually lived there and he didn't feel that way at all. Yet, here the man was, protecting him, giving him the benefit of the doubt. He made himself meet Ollie's eyes. He nodded and held out his hand so they could shake on it.

Ollie picked up the piece Whit had wadded and tossed to the ground. "Well, then. Dr. Whitaker said to take these down and carry them to the Education Building. She also said you'd better have yourself a good story about where you disappeared to when that storm came over." He loaded another canvas into the wheelbarrow, careful to stack them so that no more damage was done. "Volunteers are going to blow these with a hair dryer."

Whit lifted his eyebrows. "You think that'll work?"

"Don't know. Won't hurt to try."

Oh sure, Whit thought. More good press for the zoo. I mean you couldn't buy this kind of publicity. Elephant dies. Employees erect a memorial. That gets rained out. Volunteers rush to the rescue.

It was all about overcoming obstacles. Vivian had to be pleased about that.

After Whit and Ollie filled the wheel barrow, Whit delivered the load to the Education Building, where a team of volunteers laid the pieces out on long tables and set right to work with hair dryers they had brought from home.

Maybe it would work. Whit wasn't sure.

What he was sure about was that nothing would bring back Millie. Not volunteers or a hair dryer or anything. The elephant was gone for good.

On his way back with the empty wheelbarrow, he

stopped off at Savannah Point. The giraffes had moved away from the building where they had huddled before the rain and were now strolling in their awkward way along the back fence line. Jakari, who was barely a year old, stretched his tongue toward the leaf sack suspended by the keepers just out of his reach. Whit almost couldn't believe how much the little guy had grown since he was born. Whit had seen lots of animal births, but none quite like Jakari's.

For one thing his mother, Jalani, didn't moan or scream. She just paced around, then plop, out dropped a tiny giraffe. It was frightening to see the brand-new creature fall nearly seven feet to the ground. But within minutes all fear was eased as Jakari stirred and lifted himself to his wet, wobbly hooves.

"He's grown, hasn't he?" Whit turned his head toward the voice. It was his mother. He braced for the blast that was surely coming.

"Listen, Whit . . . Connie told me what happened today." Her eyes were steely but her voice was resigned. "You know the rules. And what were you thinking, walking into someone else's house? To get a gun?!" She shook her head. "I don't even have the energy to deal with this right now. It's just not like you, Whit." She paused. "Something else: This morning I got a call. From someone who called herself 'Bird Girl.' Does she have anything to do with this gun fiasco?"

Whit sucked in his breath. "Stella? Really?"

Vivian wrinkled her brow. "That's what she said. Then when I said I was your mother and would give you a message, she hung up."

Whit's heart was like a soap bubble that was getting bigger and bigger. Stella had called him. She knew he'd be worried, and she'd called to let him know what was going on. He couldn't blame her for hanging up on his mother. She could be pretty intimidating.

"Mom, was there anything else? Did she say anything else?"

"I don't think so. But I don't know." She shook her head. "Nothing she said made any sense. And then Doc handed me the tiger cubs' latest lab reports—I don't know. That's all I can remember."

Whit gritted his teeth. How could she not listen to Stella? How could she not know how important it was?

Vivian patted him on the back, completely oblivious to his anger. "Well, best get back to it. I'll see you at the Lodge later."

Whit waited until she was out of sight before punching the air and letting out a little scream. It was so frustrating! He would give anything to talk with Stella. So much had happened since he'd seen her last. If her day had been half as eventful as his, it would take them hours to catch up.

He turned from the giraffe enclosure and lifted the handles of the wheelbarrow. Stella had called. It was the best news he'd had all day. And it's not like he had given her his phone number. To call him, she would've had to search for it. Which required time. And effort.

Whit whistled as he hauled three more loads of Millie's art to the Education Building. When he got tired of whistling, he hummed a tune that sounded like carousel music.

19 ❋ ZEBRA WHISPERER

The next few days crawled by, with no more rain and no word from Stella. The buzz Whit had experienced when Stella called him was gone, yet he couldn't say what exactly he was hoping for. He wished he could verbalize his hope the way his mother did when she very clearly said, "I hope we break our attendance record on the Fourth of July." Or the way Tony did just a week after Millie's death when he said, "I hope Wanda and Lila stop bickering. It's like they don't know how to handle each other without Millie in the enclosure."

Whit's hope wasn't as concrete as that. Well, it was and it wasn't. He hoped he would see the Bird Girl again. He hoped she was okay. But there was another hope, one that went much deeper. Ever since his mother told him about the phone call from Stella, he'd been thinking about that word *escape*.

The latest escape story at Meadowbrook Zoo involved Elvis the king cobra. Five days ago the snake had slithered down the drainpipe that his keeper accidentally left unplugged after cleaning its cage. More likely the cobra was curious. Or cold. Or craving darkness.

Well, he got all three. Elvis still had not been recovered, and Vivian had fielded at least a half a dozen calls a day from neighbors who were sure it was the zoo's snake under the house or in the bathtub. So far, it hadn't been the king cobra. It had been just regular Alabama brown rat snakes most likely looking for water.

There hadn't been another drop of rain since the short shower that came the day of Millie's death. According to Channel 6, the drought was now in Stage 3. And with the Fourth of July holiday coming so soon, city officers had put an official ban on fireworks of any kind. No sparklers, no bottle caps, no hotdogs on sticks and held over a bonfire. Whit was disappointed because he always loved watching the fireworks put on by the zoo. It was the busiest day all year in terms of zoo attendance, and the fireworks were always the grand finale. But not this year.

Every day since the day the police came and took

away Phil's gun, Whit had made the journey across the road and through the Botanical Gardens to check on Stella. But so far the Taylors' door stayed locked and the windows dark. He always spent a few minutes with Poppy, rubbing his belly and scratching behind his ears. And then Juan Carlos would come out. He said he always knew when Whit was there by the way he knocked on Stella's door.

The yo-yo, Whit learned, had a name. Juan Carlos called it Fred. Whit laughed when he told him, and after that, part of their time together was Juan Carlos teaching him how to work with Fred. But Whit didn't think he'd ever be as good at it as Juan Carlos was.

The whole thing with Stella had begun to feel hazy, like it had never even happened. But it *had* happened. Whit knew it had because he got mad every time some other zoo guest dared sit on the bench in front of Flamingo Island. And when he sat on the carousel by himself at night, his eyes got itchy and he had to clear his throat. He played the images of her over and over again, until they were memorized.

She had to come back. She *had* to.

Meanwhile, the little city of Meadowbrook Zoo continued its patterns of sleep and wake, feed and clean.

Whit couldn't bring himself to pick up the digital recorder with no subject to study, so he threw himself into finishing a different home-school project—a study of the nesting habits of raptors. It gave him an excuse to sit in the dark of the Predator House where it was nice and cool. It was a safe place for him to relax and sort things out in his mind as he watched the pair of bald eagles.

On the second afternoon of his new project, Ms. Connie joined him. "Any surprising observations?" she asked. "Any revelations?"

Whit stretched out his legs and sighed. He had a feeling she wasn't just asking him about the birds. "If I was an artist like Stella, I'd draw them." He thought they'd make great subjects because they didn't move much, except for their eyes. The yellow eyes cocked and swiveled, constantly scanning the enclosure.

"You don't have to be an artist to draw, Whit. Give it a shot. What's the worst thing that can happen?"

"Um, I could draw a really awful bird?" Drawing had never been Whit's thing. He was clumsy with a pencil and had always preferred using a keyboard.

"And the world would not come crashing to a halt, I promise you that."

He gave her a sideways glance. So many things had

happened lately that proved that to be true. The world just kept on spinning even on the days he wished it wouldn't. "Ms. Connie?" He forced his mind back to the project. "What do you think these eagles would be like in the wild?" The video footage he'd seen of wild eagles showed their struggle against the elements, but it also showed how much time and energy they spent hunting and eating live prey.

At the zoo the eagles got dead fish and rats and chicks sprinkled with vitamin supplements, which probably lengthened their lives. Yet where was the joy for captive eagles? The more he thought about it, the more he thought Phil might have a point. In some ways it was cruel to keep animals in enclosures.

"They'd be different," Ms. Connie said. "Everything is at least a little influenced by environment."

"I guess so," Whit conceded. Maybe he would suggest some improvements to the eagles' environment. Maybe the eagles would be his mother's next big fundraising project and they could create an enclosure that more closely mimicked their natural habitat.

Or maybe, since the fireworks had been canceled, they could feature the eagles on the Fourth of July. Whit couldn't remember the last time the zoo had done a Birds of Prey show. Guests always seemed to like getting up close and personal with the regal birds, even if their talons were so dangerous the keeper had to wear thick leather gloves that went all the way up the arm.

His thoughts shifted again, back to Stella. "You know the incident with the gun?" He swallowed as he realized he was about to tell one of Stella's secrets. But he needed to. He *had* to. "Phil—Stella's father—had an accident with that gun. He shot his own son. In the leg."

Whit watched Ms. Connie's face closely for any signs of panic or fear or shock. But all she did was lift her eyebrows. "Scary, isn't it? From what Rosa told me, things have not been good at Stella's house for a long time. There are problems there, Whit. Problems bigger than a gun or even you and me." She grabbed his chin to make him look at her. "I know you miss Stella. And I know you're trying to make sense of things." She let go of his chin, but her eyes held his. "But some things don't make sense no matter how many times you turn them over in your mind." She leaned in as a large group of Zoo Campers came into the building. "No one— not even your parents—are the key to your happiness.

You've got to find that—" She tapped his chest with her finger. "In here."

The kids swarmed around them making conversation impossible, so Ms. Connie waved to Whit and headed for the door. Whit waved back and greeted Hannah.

Hannah gathered the kids and gave him a big smile. "Thank goodness you're here." She turned back to the children. "Kids, this is Whit. His parents work here, so Whit lives at the zoo all year round. If there's anyone who can answer your question, it's this guy."

The children crowded around Whit, their name-tags dancing as the kids jostled, each child trying to get the best view of him. As if he were a Level One animal brought out for them to examine and touch, instead of a regular boy.

Whit tolerated it for a minute, then held his hands up and backed away. "I don't know. These creatures look vicious."

Hannah grinned again when the children laughed. "They want to know which animal in the zoo has the biggest appetite."

"Well, that's easy, Hannah." Whit made his eyes big and curved his fingers into claws. "The *children*." Of course, all the kids squealed.

The campers had no idea it was a well-rehearsed script. Hannah and Whit had been performing that stunt ever since Whit turned nine years old. And it was true, sort of. Guests did consume a whole lot of popcorn and ice cream and hamburgers from Safari Joe's. And Hannah would tell them about how an elephant can consume more than a hundred pounds of hay daily, plus twenty-five pounds of fruits and veggies. And if it were Millie, a whole bunch of monkey chow, too.

As Hannah continued to entertain the kids with animal facts, Whit backed away. He was just about to head down the sidewalk when Hannah's walkie-talkie crackled. "Joe DiMaggio. I repeat, Joe DiMaggio."

Hannah met his gaze as she pressed the button to reply. "Affirmative. Location?"

Whit barely breathed as they waited for the reply to come across the walkie-talkie. Escapes always made his heart pound. The unpredictable nature of it was strangely exciting. Sure, there was danger. But there were plans in place, protocol. It was like being on the inside of a criminal investigation.

Finally the report came. "Grévy's zebra. Over and out."

Hannah threw up her hands then launched into her spiel about the bald eagle. Procedures varied depending on the location of the campers when an escape was reported. Since they were currently safe in a building, Hannah's job was to keep them there until the animal was recovered, or until other instructions came across the walkie-talkie. But those rules didn't apply to Whit.

He waved to Hannah as casually as possible. "Guess I'll go then. Bye, kids." As he strolled out, he puzzled over the report: Grévy's zebra. The hoofed animals weren't usually the escape artists. In fact, it almost never happened.

The good news was that it wasn't one of the big cats. Or a bear. Now, that would have been disastrous. And Hannah would have had to rush the kids to the Education Building, all the while not acting as if they were rushing at all. Vivian had very specific procedures in place for each potential escapee, and the employees were drilled weekly so that they'd always be ready.

The safety of the guests—and the employees—depended on it.

As Whit made his way out of the Predator House, he couldn't quite recall the protocol for zebras. And when he stepped into the midday heat, it was if his brain powered off. Heck, it must be close to 100 degrees! And even with the cover of wisteria vines, the intensity made him long for the days when he could toddle around the zoo in his swimming trunks.

Good thing zebras are well adapted to heat, Whit thought. This was probably nothing compared to what conditions were like on the African plain.

Whit passed the wooden walkway that marked the entrance to Sugarland Swamp, where the alligators lazed on the creek banks, their eyes half open. He sure hoped the zebra didn't go in there. Fourteen-foot Hank would probably be thrilled to latch on to something so eye-catching. But more than likely the bayou music that poured from the speakers would be enough to keep the zebra away.

Whit peered down the sidewalk. It was full of guests, but there wasn't a zoo employee in sight. Even the ice-cream cart was closed down. Whit knew this was because of the Joe DiMaggio. The whole place went into emergency mode, and Vivian relied on the staff to help contain the animal. And to keep it a secret from the public. The last thing anyone needed was some big panic to sweep through the place. No telling what the animals would do if the guests started raising a ruckus.

For the billionth time Whit wished he had a staff walkie-talkie. Or a cell phone, like everyone else had these days. Then he'd know what was going on. As it was, he'd have to backtrack to his secret spot by the Reptile House. Because of the way the building was positioned on top of a small hill, he could stand on his tiptoes and see almost all of the zoo grounds.

Just as he was passing Flamingo Island, Whit heard Ferdinand scream. He followed the sound and immediately saw the reason for the peacock's alarm.

There, in the patch of pine trees between the Reptile House and Lorikeet Landing was the zebra. And walking toward the zebra as if she were some sort of zebra whisperer was Stella.

20 ✿ THE FIRST-AID STATION

"Stella!" he called, as the zoo staff closed in behind the zebra. He was careful to keep his voice low. Even though the zebra was calm as Stella approached, Whit knew how quickly that could change. One minute you think you're dealing with a docile animal, the next it's attacking you.

When Stella turned her head, her hair swung out and caught the sunlight. For a split second, she looked like an angel. Then everything went terribly wrong.

Gigi the zebra, reared and pawed the air with its front hooves. Whit imagined those hooves coming down on Stella, and he bolted toward her. "Get out of the way!"

Gigi spun away from Stella. But Stella didn't run as he'd hoped. Instead she dropped to the ground and curled herself into a ball exactly like one of those fire drill videos.

Gigi snorted and pinned back her ears. The zebra

dipped her head and charged Vivian and the zebra keepers. Doc didn't even flinch. He held the gun steady and pulled the trigger to release the anesthetic dart.

The needle hit the zebra right in the chest, but it probably didn't even notice the prick as it plowed into the crowd of zoo staff, knocking Vivian off her feet. Whit looked at Stella, then his mother, and didn't know what to do. They were both sprawled out on the ground. After a few minutes of wobbly steps, the zebra was on the ground, too.

As the keepers moved in to secure the animal with a horse halter and some rope, Whit rushed to Stella's side. He touched her arm. "Are you okay?"

She nodded, tears filling her eyes.

"Nothing broken or anything?"

She tested her arms and legs. "Really, I'm okay."

Whit wanted to ask her what she was thinking, approaching a wild animal like that. He wanted to know where she had been and when did she get back. But it would all have to wait until later. Because Vivian was still on the ground.

She held her left wrist in her right hand while Doc used his fingers to examine the injury. Whit didn't need Doc to tell him that the arm was broken.

His mother's face was flushed and her movements were slow, but she picked herself up and offered a faltering smile. "Everyone back to work," she said, and leaned against Doc. "Right, Doc? I'll get a cast put on, and in six weeks I'll be good as new."

Doc nodded reassuringly, and the staff dispersed quickly. They knew Vivian would want the atmosphere at the zoo to return to normal just as soon as possible.

Vivian turned next to the small group of onlookers who had gathered during the excitement. She couldn't be sure what exactly they had witnessed, so, before she could see to her arm, she had to do a little public relations work. Her voice wavered as she continued. "Doc, see to our young guest, will you?" She watched as Doc hurried to Stella, then scanned the crowd. "And where are the girl's parents?"

People whispered and looked from one to the other, but neither Phil nor Mrs. Taylor was anywhere to be seen. Whit knew that wouldn't look good to the guests, so he blurted an explanation. "They stopped to get a drink at Safari Joe's. They should be here any minute."

When Vivian gave Whit a forced smile, his throat tightened. She was really in pain.

"Thank you, Whit." His mother smiled again, broader this time. "Ladies and gentlemen, thank you for your patience. Everything is under control now. Our zebra friend here just got a little overexcited today and jumped the fence." Vivian lowered her voice and put her fingers to her mouth as if she was telling a secret. "She's in heat, you know."

The crowd tittered, and Vivian turned to Doc and Stella. "How's the young lady after her zebra encounter?"

Doc pulled his stethoscope from his ears. "Just fine, Dr. Whitaker. Let's get both of you to the first-aid station."

The first-aid station was a tiny room in the corner of the Education Building. It was stocked with Band-Aids and hydrogen peroxide and Benadryl. There was also a refrigerator with some antivenom in case of staff snakebites, but that was just an extra precaution. There was another station in the Reptile House, and if it ever happened—which it hadn't—that's where it would most likely be administered.

Inside, Vivian was a different person. Whit cringed as she barked orders over the walkie-talkie. He took a quick look at Stella, but she wouldn't meet his eye. She hadn't said a word to him on the walk over, and Whit didn't know what to think. He just wanted to get this part over with, the scolding from his mother. Then he and Stella could go somewhere and talk it out. Alone. Without zebras or other humans.

As soon as Vivian set down the walkie-talkie, she winced. She groaned as she lifted her arm. "Doc is going to drive me to the emergency room so they can set the broken bone. I need you to stay here. Do you understand me? I need to know you're where you're supposed to be."

Whit nodded. Vivian always got like this after an animal escape. It was like a ball of yarn unraveling, and she'd scurry in to wind it back up again. She'd be like this for a day or two, then her mind would shift to other things, and Whit would be forgotten again.

Vivian turned to Stella. "You're sure you're okay then?" Stella nodded, but didn't say anything. "And your parents are on their way?"

Stella shrugged. "Not exactly. They don't know I'm here."

"Mom," Whit said quickly. "This is Stella. My friend. Remember?"

Vivian cocked her head and held Whit's gaze. "Of

course I remember." She reached out her good hand. "Very nice to meet you, Stella." Her eyes brightened. "I think a brave girl like you deserves a free Family Pass after all you've been through today. Would you like that?"

"Yes ma'am. But we already have a Family Pass. That's how I can come every day."

"Every day, huh?" Vivian looked from Whit to Stella, suspicion making her eyes squinty. "And you two see each other every day?"

"Yep." Whit was so proud he was about to bust. Even though it wasn't true. He hadn't seen Stella in two weeks. But he figured every day she came to the zoo, yep, he saw her.

Doc cleared his throat. "Dr. Whitaker, we really should be going."

After they said their goodbyes and the door closed behind them, Whit and Stella were alone. The room seemed larger, and after all the commotion of the zebra escape and capture, the quiet was awkward.

Whit scratched his head. "So . . ."

Stella grinned. "So what?"

"I'm really glad to see you. Finally. I wasn't sure you were ever coming back."

She shrugged, her smile shy. "Here I am."

He grinned, then scratched his cheek as his mood turned serious. "So, what were you doing out there? Why did you go up to the zebra like that?"

Her smile disappeared and she looked at the sparkling tile. Vivian said even though the first-aid station wasn't used all that often, it was really important that it make an impression of health and safety. Stella chewed her lip. "I don't know. It just seemed like the thing to do. It was just like in *Black Stallion* when they're on the deserted beach and Alec feeds the Black seaweed."

"Is that before or after the Black crushes out the snake and saves Alec's life?"

She giggled. "You *would* like that part."

"Yep. That's when you know they really are friends. When the horse risks his own life to save his friend."

She shoved her hands in her pockets. "I just thought it would be cool. You know, to make friends with a wild animal."

Whit blew out through his nose and shook his head. "I can't believe you put yourself in danger like that."

Her eyes got shiny, as if she might cry. "I don't know. It was stupid. I do stupid things sometimes."

"You're not stupid." Whit fished the lighter out of

his pocket and held it out to her. "I'm just glad you're okay. I was tired of talking to Phil's lighter."

She giggled. "What about your digital recorder? Don't you still have it?"

"Well, sure I do. But there's been nothing to report. My subject has been gone for so long."

Stella rolled the lighter between her palms. "I don't even know why I bothered to take this stupid lighter. Would you believe it didn't stop him from smoking for more than half an hour? All he did was yell for Mama to run down to the Piggly Wiggly and get another one."

Mrs. Taylor could have said no, Whit thought to himself. Wasn't that one of the benefits of being a grown-up?

"Just tell me what happened. It can't be any worse than all the things I've imagined."

She rubbed her forehead as if she had a headache. "When I got home that morning, Mama was sitting in the kitchen with her head on the table and the phone in her lap. My grandmother died."

"Your grandmother?"

Stella nodded. "My father's mother. In Mobile."

"Wow." Whit ran his hands through his hair again. "That's awful."

"I know. Mama was just praying I'd get home safe so she wouldn't have to tell Phil that his mother was dead *and* his daughter was missing." Stella tucked her hair behind her ears. "Mama said if it had been twenty more minutes she would have called the police."

"So you didn't get in trouble about staying gone the whole night? I mean, with Phil?"

She pressed her lips together and shook her head. "And he was so different when we were in Mobile. Like Grandmother's death made him want to pull himself together. He even held Mama's hand at the funeral." She swallowed. "But since we got home, he's been worse than ever. Shouting and throwing things—he freaked out when he couldn't find his gun."

Whit's eyes widened. "You mean the one from under his chair?" As if there was another one.

Her voice cracked. "He accused Mama of stealing it. He said when he finds it she's going to be sorry."

Now Phil was threatening to hurt Stella's mother. And Stella seemed more distraught than ever. He wasn't at all sure anymore that he had done the right thing.

"But—" He didn't know what to say. He couldn't

believe Juan Carlos and his family hadn't told them what happened. Then again, why would they, when Phil was so unpredictable? Maybe they were more like his mother than he thought. Maybe they didn't like being involved in the Taylor family's personal business, either.

Whit wasn't sure if he should tell her about the gun. "I thought that was Hugo's plan, to get rid of the gun. I thought that would be a *good* thing."

"I know. I haven't even told Hugo yet. He's going to be so mad."

Whit wanted to hit something. It wasn't enough to have made the situation with Phil even worse. Nope, he had to make Hugo mad, too. "Can't your mother do something? I mean, can't she report him or something? To the police? For threatening her?"

Tears made her face glisten in the fluorescent light. "Whit, I don't know! She won't talk to me about it. Mama said I'm better off at the zoo today. She said to let her handle it."

Whit was quiet as he watched her. She'd been through so much in the time they'd been apart. Here he'd been feeling so sorry for himself, missing her, feeling so forgotten, when she'd been dealing with her grandmother's death. And now with Phil's reaction to the missing gun.

Clearly he hadn't thought the whole thing through when he had decided to take the gun. But it had to be the right thing. It *had* to be. Phil had no business with the gun, even if it wasn't according to Hugo's schedule. They were all a lot safer now that the gun was gone.

He put his arms around her instead, the way a big brother would. "What about Hugo? Did you see him when you were in Mobile?"

She shook her head, and he could smell smoke in her hair, and just the faintest scent of apple shampoo. He couldn't think of a single thing to say as she trembled and cried, so he just held her like that until she pulled away.

"I thought for sure he'd come to the funeral. Mama thought so, too." She wiped her eyes. "Finally the day after the funeral he called. He said he wanted to see us, but he couldn't come. Not with Phil there."

"I'm just glad you're okay." Whit puzzled over it all as he handed her a tissue. He didn't understand Hugo. How could he let them go back with Phil? He couldn't imagine choosing not to see Stella whenever the opportunity arose. Hugo had to know how much he meant to his sister.

Before he said anything foolish, Whit decided it was probably better just to stick to his own feelings. So he told her how disappointed he was when he went to her house only to find she still wasn't there. "The good news is I've gotten to know Juan Carlos. And Poppy."

Stella's eyes brightened. "Yeah, I heard. Juan Carlos said you're getting better with Fred."

Whit laughed. He liked it so much when she teased him. "Yep. You're gonna be so impressed." Whit pretended to yo-yo, and Stella giggled.

Something about her giggle reminded Whit of the last time he'd seen her, and that reminded him of Millie. Stella had been one of the last people to see Millie alive. "Hey, did you hear what happened? To Millie, I mean."

This time it was Stella who reached out to Whit. "We heard it on the radio when we were driving that day to Mobile. It must have been awful."

Whit thought back to that day, to his conversation with Tony in the Elephant House when Millie was still laid out on the floor. There was no way to describe it.

And he didn't want to anyway. Stella had enough sadness to deal with without adding Whit's to the heap.

"Yep, it was terrible." He swallowed, then looked her straight in the eyes. "But things are better now. If Wanda and Lila would stop quarreling, it would be just about perfect."

"Perfect?" She play-punched him in the arm. "I thought you hated the zoo."

Whit grinned and rubbed the spot on the top of his arm where her fist had touched. "Well, I don't hate it when you're here. Besides what's to hate on a day when there's two Joe DiMaggio's? You've got to admit the whole zebra thing was pretty cool. And you know we've still got an escaped snake. That provides for a little entertainment."

Whit expected her to smile, but she didn't. Her face had that faraway look that he'd seen so many times on his mother. Something was on her mind. He was about to ask her what it was when she hopped up out of her chair, eyes urgent. "Whit, do you like me? I mean really like me?"

Whit twisted his watch strap round and round on his wrist. "Well, sure I do, Stella. You know that. I've been crazy with worry all this time without you."

She licked her lips. "Well, I need you to do something for me. I need you to take me back to the carousel. And this time when the sun comes up, I don't want to leave."

"What do you mean?"

"Just what I said. And what Mama said. I'm better off here than at home. So what I want you to do is hide me. Hide me in the zoo."

21 ❋ TRAIN RIDE

Ollie pushed through the door to the first-aid station before Whit had a chance to respond to Stella.

"Got ourselves a scraped knee," he said, and motioned to a small boy and his father to come inside. "Don't you worry, little fella." Ollie patted the boy on his head, as if he really enjoyed this part of his job. "We'll get you fixed up in no time."

Whit pressed his back against the wall, once again aware of how small the first-aid station actually was. "We'll just get out of your way then." He pulled Stella toward the door, then paused before making his exit. He remembered a few weeks ago, how mad his mother was after Ollie doled out Band-Aids and peroxide without recording every single detail in the log. Vivian said it was a lawsuit waiting to happen.

"Hey, Ollie," Whit said, thinking about how pale

his mother looked before she went to the hospital. She really didn't need any more trouble today. "Want me to write everything down for you?" It was the least he could do.

Ollie popped on a pair of latex gloves. "I got it."

Whit nodded. Ollie was so confident and capable. He guessed that was one good thing that came from working at the zoo for so long. He held the door open for Stella.

The heat was staggering, like running into a wall. Whit waited for a wave of dizziness to pass. Was it the heat that made him feel so light-headed, or was it Stella? He replayed her words in his head: *Hide me in the zoo.*

Did she really mean it? It was so hard to tell. And it's not like he could ask her. Not here, with a million people around. Heck, he could barely keep up with her, much less *talk*.

Whit made himself jog, even though it made his head feel worse. "What are you in such a hurry for?"

She flipped back her hair, so that it all hung down her back. "I want to see the bears, that's all." The way she said it, Whit could tell it wasn't really about the bears. Whatever was going on with her was far more significant.

As Stella examined the sign in front of the enclosure that held the Bornean sun bears, Whit's mind turned like the carousel. What if he *did* hide her at the zoo? The thought made him feel like a bandit waiting behind a rock for the bank coach to round the bend. He knew just what Billy the Kid would do to that bandit, if he could catch him. He knew how Ms. Connie would react, too. When they'd done their unit on the Westward Expansion, she'd said it was important to remember how men are defined by the times they live in. Sometimes the bad guys aren't all bad. Sometimes it's just a bad situation.

Whit thought pretty much anyone would agree that Stella's situation was bad.

But to *hide* her . . . where would he even put her? No way could he get away with that for more than a night. If they did it, they would need to have a plan for where to go next. She couldn't just live at the zoo like one of the animals. It was such a public place that it wouldn't work.

Whit shoved the thought aside. They would figure it out. But right now he wanted to just talk to her and enjoy her company. There would be time for all that serious stuff later.

He pressed against the enclosure glass, until he spied the bear. It was high up in the tree, all stretched out. "Its name comes from that yellow crescent on its chest." He pointed, so she could see what he was talking about.

Stella craned her neck. "Looks like he's trying to get a suntan or something."

"Yep, they're nocturnal. Pretty much all they do during the day is sleep."

"Do they eat berries like other bears?"

"Sometimes. They like insects and lizards, fruits and veggies. Here we feed them bear chow mostly. It's easier, and Doc can be sure they get all the vitamins and minerals they need."

"I wish I could draw him."

"But he's not a bird."

She giggled. "I know. I should probably draw something else, don't you think?"

"I like your birds. But if you wanted to branch out, this guy would be a good choice. Better draw him while you can."

"Why do you say that?"

"Don't you know?" Whit pointed to the sign in front of the exhibit. "Sun bears are like one of the most endangered species we have here."

"How come I've never heard of them?" Whit hated to admit it, but he liked knowing the answers to her questions. It made him feel smart and important, like all these years spent at the zoo hadn't been for nothing. "They just aren't flashy enough to get a lot of attention. And they're kind of boring. My mother always says they lead secret lives."

Stella folded her arms against her chest. "I won't draw them then. If they want to be kept secret, then I won't be the one to tell."

Whit smiled, and his head felt normal again. This was the Stella he remembered.

"Stella," he began. In a way she was his secret. He wanted to tell her he'd do anything for her.

She pulled on his arm. "Let's go ride the train."

"Okay." Whit smiled. "But we'll have to get tokens."

"But you're like royalty here. Why do you have to get a token?"

Whit leaned in close to her ear as a family walked

past. "Vivian says it wouldn't look right. So I just go to the token window and pretend I'm just like everyone else. Only all the employees know me, so I don't actually have to pay any money."

"Wow. Your mom thinks of everything, doesn't she?"

He got an image of his mom with her forced smile and broken arm. "Everything that has to do with the zoo."

"So, did you get in trouble? After the night on the carousel?"

"Nope. Everyone was so busy with Millie . . . they never even noticed I was gone."

"Wow. See, we could hide out together and no one would ever need to know."

Whit started to laugh, but when he looked at Stella's face, it was completely serious. She really wanted to run away. She really believed it could work. And she wanted him to go with her.

He pointed the way to the train token counter. All of a sudden her problems seemed bigger than his problems, bigger than *him*. He didn't quite know what to do with the feeling. So he decided to let it go. It was too beautiful a day to think about running away and hiding out.

He just wanted things to be normal, fun, smooth. And he wanted to ride the train with Stella. Ever since the first day he saw her sitting on that bench in front of Flamingo Island he'd imagined riding with her in one of those little cars, showing her all the little secret things about the zoo that regular people never noticed.

By the time they got their tokens and made their way to the gate, the train was nearly loaded. The conductor was just latching the gate when he saw that it was Whit coming up the walkway. "Just in time, Whit."

Whit flashed him a smile, then headed for the one open seat near the middle of the train. It was always like that—the front and back filled up the fastest, then the middle. It had never much mattered to Whit. He'd sit anywhere.

The whistle blew and they were off. They rode in silence at first, as the kids in front of them squealed about every animal they passed. Whit had heard it all before, many times, but it was still fun to feel the guests' excitement.

As the train crawled through the empty woods that might someday be cleared for other animal exhibits, Whit closed his eyes and let the breeze cool his face and arms. He could feel Stella beside him, could even hear her breathing. This is what it's like to be alive, he thought. Nothing else mattered more than the fact that the Bird Girl was here. She came back to the zoo to see *him*.

Whit's eyes popped open when the train entered the tunnel. "I know!" He cupped his hand against his mouth and whispered in her ear. "You can stay in the barn. No one will ever notice you there."

"The barn? Like over near the carousel?"

Whit nodded. "There's a cellar there, lined in bales of hay. It's the perfect spot."

When they came out of the tunnel they were both smiling. It was like going back in time to the first day he saw her. The world felt rich and ripe with possibility. Here they were, at the Meadowbrook Zoo, on a little red train with laughing children all around. Whit understood for the first time why more people came to the zoo than to all other sporting events combined.

It wasn't for the animals. Not really. It was for moments like this one.

People went to the zoo to share time with each other, to smile the way he and Stella were smiling as the train chugged into the station.

22 ❋ PROMISE

Whit and Stella floated through the rest of the day like a couple of balloons accidentally let loose from a child's pudgy palm. Not like zoo balloons, which were weighted. Regular ones. They even got balloons, one blue and one yellow, and tied them to their wrists. They explored every exhibit in the zoo, some more than once. When they got to Savannah Point, it was feeding time for the giraffes.

"Watch," Whit whispered as the keeper spoke to the crowd of sweaty guests. "It's the best part."

The keeper held a piece of iceberg lettuce to Camille, the oldest giraffe. First she licked the keeper's hand. Then her tongue zipped out like a snake and wrapped around the treat. As Camille tucked it into her mouth and began to chew, Whit continued his private presentation in Stella's ear. "See how sweet she is? The keepers think she likes the salty flavor of skin."

Stella kept her eyes on the giraffes. "Their tongues are so long! And dark. I wasn't expecting that. It's like watching a turtle stretch its neck out the whole way. It's almost weird."

"I know. Can you imagine having an eighteen-inch tongue?"

Stella shook her head. "But I'd kill for those eyelashes."

Whit took a quick look at Stella's eyelashes. They were thick and dark brown. "Those giraffes don't have a thing on you."

"But giraffes are your favorite animal."

"Yep. If you're talking about zoo animals."

She sniffed the air. "Too bad you can't hide me with the giraffes. I bet it can get pretty smelly in the barn."

Whit nodded. "Careful or I'll banish you to the Reptile House." Reptile urine was the *worst*.

Stella looked up at the clouds gathering in the sky. "Think it'll rain?"

Whit looked up, too. It reminded him of the day he'd first gone looking for Stella, but the clouds seemed to be moving faster. "Nope. Whatever it is, it'll pass right over."

"Wouldn't it be great if it rained and they decided we could have fireworks after all?"

Whit didn't say anything but he knew it was just wishful thinking. He remembered how the rain from that one little afternoon shower had all but disappeared. And it hadn't made a dent in the drought. "Channel 6 says we're behind like eighteen inches for the year. Rodney said we might never catch up."

Stella was quiet as the clouds raced across the sky. "What time does the zoo close?"

Whit pulled out his watch. At five o'clock. "Twenty minutes."

"Then what?"

"Then the keepers muck the stalls and put the animals to bed. And we get you situated in the barn."

She smiled and leaned into him. "I'm so glad I don't have to go home. The way Phil was acting when I left—" She shook her head, as if to clear it. "It's like that gun means more to him than anything else."

Whit leaned away from her. This whole time he'd forgotten about the gun. He'd just shoved the whole thing out of his mind, as if it didn't happen. "Will your mother be okay? I mean, without the gun, Phil is mostly just noise, right?"

He wanted more than anything for it to be like the time he had been in charge of Nut Nut when a school group came in for a field trip. Somehow the bird got loose in the Activity Hall, and she used her beak and toes to climb the walled art display into the rafters. His mother was furious, and the school was irritated because first, it wasn't sanitary, and second, it was such a distraction. Vivian would have moved the group to the outdoor amphitheater, but it was raining that day. For hours Nut Nut perched on the rafters, calling her name to the kids as they passed. Finally the bird got hungry enough and climbed down to Whit's outstretched hand.

Whit still remembered how all the kids clapped and cheered. It made him feel like a hero, like he'd done something really important. And that's how he wanted the story to go about how he'd taken the gun away from Phil.

Stella had no way of knowing what Whit wanted from her. "You know what?" She pushed her hair behind her shoulders. "I'm tired of talking about it. I'm tired of thinking about it. I just want to pretend this is all there is—a zoo and a boy named Whit."

When Stella said his name, it wasn't just some throwaway syllable. She made him feel so . . . special.

Which is why he forced the other thoughts out of his mind—thoughts about Stella's mother and Phil and his own part in all the drama.

He thought about his own mother, too. He hadn't seen her again since she left for the hospital. He wanted her to be okay. .

As the remaining guests made their way toward the front gates to exit the zoo, Whit and Stella walked the opposite way, toward the playground, where they sat on the carousel while the keepers finished up in the barn. Whit knew the routine practically by heart from the home-school unit he'd done on Alabama farm animals. First they filled the hay bags, fed the animals in the yards, then put down fresh shavings in the stalls.

They brought the cow in first and milked her. She was a Jersey cow with a velvety brown nose—not one of those black and white Holsteins. Before they built and stocked the barn, Whit didn't even know cows came in colors other than black and white. For all his parents' trips to Africa, they didn't spend much time on domesticated animals. Heck, Whit had never even had a dog or cat or goldfish. So the arrival of the calf was a big deal and one of the few animals at the zoo

Whit was actually allowed to play with. He christened her Penny and laughed whenever she would follow him around, nudging him in the rear end.

Whit looked at his watch. "They're running slow tonight."

She shrugged her shoulders. "It's okay. At least no one's shouting at me or asking stupid questions."

"What stupid questions?"

Stella rolled her eyes. "Well, when I was in Mobile, they all kept asking me, 'What do you want to be when you grow up?'"

"Well, what *do* you want to be?"

She shrugged again, her shoulders saying "I don't know" without the need of words. "The only answer that kept popping into my head was, 'Not like you.' But that wouldn't go over so well."

Whit lifted his eyebrows. Nope, he couldn't imagine that going over very well with anyone.

"Look," Whit said, and pointed as the pigs came next, in all their grunting glory. The pair was almost too large for the pen, which meant that soon the pigs would have to be replaced with smaller ones. It wasn't something his mother liked to make public, but just like on a regular farm it was best not to get too attached. Not that Whit ever did. It was just interesting, that's all.

Stella scratched at her leg. As the sky darkened, the mosquitoes began their feast. "Don't worry, I'll bring you some bug spray. And a pillow. Whatever you need."

The Rhode Island red hens clucked as the keepers tossed out seed. Whit looked at Stella. "You know, when the rooster crows, it can be pretty loud. Are you sure you can handle it?"

She met his challenge with a crooked grin. "I hear my father bellow like a runaway train every morning. I don't think a rooster's going to bother me."

"Okay. But what about Ferdinand? Peacocks do more than just fan their feathers." He pointed at the peacock as he waddled by, his tail feathers tucked in tight. Whit knew he was heading for his favorite night spot, which happened to be a hydrangea bush just outside the chicken coop.

"I heard a peacock at a zoo in New York or Pennsylvania or somewhere attacked a little boy. Scratched his face." She met Whit's eyes. "Think Ferdinand would ever do something like that?"

"See, that's the thing about wild animals. You just never can tell." He sighed. "Ferdinand, he's pretty laid-back. But I still wouldn't test him, you know? That boy was teasing the peacock with a piece of peppermint candy. Holding it out, then putting it in his pocket. I mean, even a human might scratch you over something like that."

"I wish I had my sketchpad and pencils. I was in such a hurry this morning to leave, I forgot my backpack."

Whit did his Billy the Kid swagger. "Don't you fret, little lady. Me and my horse'll get you fixed right up."

"Shhh." Stella giggled as the keepers came around to close the barn doors. "It's not that big of a deal."

Whit put a finger to his lips as the keepers moved closer. He wanted to hear their conversation so they could be sure the keepers were finished for the day before going into the barn.

"See ya in the morning," one said to the other. "And, hey, don't forget to write in the report about the blown lightbulbs in the chicken coop." He fastened the latch. "You know how Dr. Whitaker is. Wants to know every little thing."

"Will do," the bearded keeper replied, and shifted the animals' daily charts from one hip to the other.

As he turned to go, he nodded toward Whit. "See ya, kid."

Whit waved. "See ya."

As soon as they were out of sight, Whit leaped up from the carousel so quick it made Stella jump. She followed close behind as he made his way around the back side of the barn. "What, are you in a hurry to get rid of me?"

Whit turned around, ready to explain that it wasn't that, not at all. It was just that he wanted it to work out. He wanted the space where he was putting her to be comfortable.

He opened his mouth, then shut it. Because her eyes were all sparkly, and that meant she was only teasing him.

Whit grinned. He still had a lot to learn about being a real friend. But Stella made it fun.

From inside the barn, the animals snorted and grunted as they settled down for the night. "As long as we get you settled before they all get to sleep, it ought to be fine. After that we run the risk of waking them up. You wouldn't believe the racket they make when they hear unusual noises at night."

He fumbled with the keypad beside the small

hidden door. "You should have heard them the time a raccoon got in. All that raccoon wanted was some corn, but man, those pigs! Started squealing like there was no tomorrow. It took forever for Gus, the night watchman, to get them all settled."

He pulled open the door. It was a store room for the shovels, rakes, and buckets and anything else the keepers used on a daily basis. The walls were lined with bales of hay, and to the left was a large wooden barrel the keepers used as a trash can. Fortunately it was only partway filled, so Whit was able to lift one side then roll it on its rim.

"No way," Stella said. In the middle of the dirt floor where the barrel used to be was a small square door. Whit pulled up the rope handle, exposing a small set of stairs, kind of like the one that led to the attic at the Lodge.

Whit waved his hand and grinned at Stella. "This is it."

She stepped on the first stair and lowered herself down step by step. When her head dipped below ground level, she looked up at Whit. "It feels kind of like crawling into a grave."

"Don't worry. It widens out down there. And it's

only for a little while—just until Gus makes his security pass. By then I'll be back with some supplies."

"Maybe if I had a flashlight. It's awfully dark."

He looked at his watch. Almost suppertime. "I'll bring you one, okay? And some blankets and some supper. Right now I need to go, but I'll be back as soon as I can."

"Could you bring some sour straws or M&M'S, too?" She bit her lip. "And maybe a pencil and some paper? That way I can draw to pass the time."

Whit nodded and made the list in his head. "What will you draw? It's not like there are any birds down there."

"Umm, rats and roaches?"

Whit laughed. "You'll be fine. And I'll be back soon. Don't worry."

Stella flashed him a smile as he slid the lid back in place. "Hurry."

"An hour, tops." Whit could still picture her face as he rolled the barrel back into place. He'd be back before she even had time to miss him. But there were a few really important things he needed to do first.

23 ❦ MADAGASCAR

When Whit came into the Lodge, he was surprised to see his mother at the stove, her arm in a purple cast and caught in a denim sling. Her eyes looked a little droopy, but she didn't appear to be in any pain.

"Just in time," Vivian said. "Spaghetti tonight. With homemade meatballs."

Tony sat at the kitchen table chopping vegetables. "And salad," he said, lifting the knife into the air, posing like a Japanese warrior.

Whit couldn't remember the last time his parents had prepared a meal. Sure, Tony was a pro at cutting vegetables because he did it every day for the elephants. But for the family? For Whit? Usually they made do with sandwiches. Or, if they were out of mayo, they ordered take-out Chinese from Golden

Palace. And special occasions were always celebrated in restaurants.

Whit puzzled over it as he washed his hands in the half bathroom. Ever since the pediatrician had suggested daily multivitamins would safeguard him against any deficiencies, his parents hadn't worried a minute over his diet. He could eat anything, or nothing. But if one of the animals were to change its habits in the slightest, his parents would be all over it faster than you could say *bacon cheeseburger*.

Back at the kitchen table, Tony was pouring a glass of wine. "Join us, Whit. Tell us about your day." He took a swallow. "I'm curious about your version of the events."

Whit's mind shuffled through all the images of the day. "You mean about the zebra?" After all the time he'd spent with Stella the zebra escape seemed like no big deal. He reminded himself that his parents hadn't seen the most exciting parts of his day: Stella on the train, Stella at the giraffe feeding, Stella on the carousel, Stella in the hole, her face aglow.

Distraction. It was still the best choice—the *only* choice, really. He didn't have anything to add about the zebra, and he wasn't willing to talk about Stella.

"Probably Mom had a more interesting day than me. How'd it go at the hospital?"

Vivian smile was wistful, as if the whole thing had happened years ago. "It was nothing more than a standard impact fracture. Clean break of both radius and ulna." She lifted her cast. "Six weeks, and I'll be good as new."

Tony reached for her good hand. "Wish I could have been at the hospital with you." Whit looked away as his father kissed her fingers. "Now that we've got Wanda and Lila all better, the staff has come down with some virus. I was by myself most of the day. And those two elephants just can't seem to get along."

Vivian pulled out a chair and sat down. "It may take them a while to establish a new routine. What have you tried?"

As Tony listed off all the ways he and the other keepers had tried to address the problem, Whit zoned out. He went through his mental list of things to take to Stella: candy, flashlight, paper and pencil.

He wasn't sure if he even had any colored pencils. Or markers. He'd have to check, just as soon as he choked down the meatballs. He was pretty sure he still had a copy of *The Guide to North American Birds*, thanks to his raptor project. Which, he remembered, he needed to finish before Ms. Connie came again next Tuesday. He just hoped everything would fit inside his backpack. Anything too large was bound to raise suspicion.

The room fell silent, and Whit realized they were done talking about the elephants. The thing to do now was to get supper over and done with so he could get back to Stella.

Vivian cleared her throat. "So, Whit." She held her fork in the air. "The reason we wanted to eat at home with you tonight was because your father and I just found out today that the money came through for the trip to Madagascar." She paused, waiting for his reaction.

When it didn't come, she set down her fork. "Well, the board is just thrilled because we'll be working with a team to help save the lemurs. And this time we want you to come with us."

The pasta in Whit's mouth turned to mush. "Madagascar? When?"

Tony cleared his throat. "Well, that's the thing. We leave July fifth. Day after tomorrow."

Whit looked from one to the other. It sounded like

a joke, but he could tell by their faces that they were serious. "But why do I have to go? You always let me stay with Ms. Connie before."

Vivian looked confused. "Wait a minute." She exchanged a look with Tony. "I thought all those other times you *wanted* to go. I thought now that you're older, it might be fun to have you along."

The chair made an awful sound as Whit pushed back from the table. "As opposed to all those other times when it wouldn't have been fun to have me along?"

Tony set his fork down. "Son, it's not like that. Lately you just seem so . . . unhappy. We thought it might cheer you up to actually get to travel with us for a change."

Whit stood in the doorway. From here they looked so small and pathetic. Like two tired, old animals. Whit wished all the employees at the zoo could see them like this. So they would know what his parents were really like. "I can't go now." Not with Stella in his life. Not with Stella in the barn. "I don't even like lemurs. I'd rather stay with Ms. Connie. Just keep things, you know, *normal*."

His mother lifted an eyebrow. "Normal, huh? Like your friend, what's her name . . . Stella?" Her eyes were bright. "The one who smells like cigarette smoke and comes to the zoo without her parents to spook the zebras? Is that the kind of normal you're looking for?"

Whit pressed his lips together. He didn't have any idea how this conversation had come to include Stella. And he sure didn't want to talk about her. It was far too risky when she was hiding out in the cellar of the barn. "I don't care what you say; I'm not going to Madagascar." Then he pulled the guilt card, the one that always worked. "If you want me to be happy, you won't make me go."

He knew he shouldn't manipulate them like that. It was just so easy. They weren't nearly as secure about their parenting decisions as they were about the zoo. But it wasn't Whit's fault he had been born. It was theirs. So if it made them uncomfortable, too bad. He didn't want to go to Madagascar. Not now.

Tony caved first, same as he always did. He covered Vivian's hand with his own then addressed Whit. "We'll see. Okay, Whit? We'll talk it over and we'll see."

Yep, you talk it over, Whit thought as he stalked off to his room. It would give him a chance to pack everything up. As he stuffed in a small blanket, he wondered how the trip had *really* come up.

Probably they had known for weeks they were going and had only just now decided to invite Whit. Zoo trips didn't generally just fall into place all of a sudden. Usually they were planned for months, down to where the traveling team would stop on the trail to pee. And on the day after the Fourth of July! That didn't make sense, either. Summers were so busy at the zoo, the Fourth in particular. Whit just couldn't shake the nagging feeling that there was more to this sudden invitation than they were telling him.

Whit checked his watch and clicked on his digital recorder. "Subject in barn for one hour already." She was probably getting pretty antsy, especially since there was no way for her to get out.

He patted under the bed for his flashlight. There was no time to waste.

24 ❋ THE BARN

Whit called her name as he tilted the barrel and rolled it away from the opening.

"You're here," she said, the relief in her voice obvious. "It's been *forever*."

An hour and a half, he wanted to say. But he was too busy getting the hatch off. When the flashlight beamed on her face, a feeling of tenderness made his eyes almost water. She was really there, like some little sister he'd been playing hide and seek with and had somehow forgotten to find. "Are you okay?"

She climbed out of the hole. "I was beginning to wonder if you were ever coming back."

Whit grinned. "You weren't scared, were you?" She had no idea how happy he was to see her. No idea at all.

"Well, it is really dark down there. I've never been so glad for a flashlight in all my life."

He opened his pack. "That's not all." He pulled out the bananas. "Your supper, little lady."

She shuddered. "Oh, I hate bananas. I hope you brought something else."

When he pulled out the box of animal crackers, she grinned. "Now that's more like it."

While Stella ate, Whit told her about his parents and the trip to Madagascar.

"Parents," she said. They were both quiet a moment as she crunched a mouthful of cookies. "But, Whit, I don't get it. Why don't you want to go? I mean, I would love to go somewhere exotic like that. Somewhere far away."

Her words hung in the air as Whit fought the lump in his throat. He *did* sort of want to go. But he couldn't tell his parents that now. And it embarrassed him to admit to Stella how much he needed her, how her friendship was the most important thing to him at the moment. He couldn't leave her. Even for a week, or however long the trip to Madagascar would take. Because school would start again in August. And Stella wouldn't come to the zoo anymore. His life would return to its mundane patterns.

Finally he turned to her. "Remember that time we threw pennies into the turtle pond?"

Stella's face softened. "Of course I remember."

"Well what was it? What did you wish for?"

"You mean before or after I knew you'd been watching me for your summer field study?"

Whit blushed as she teased. It still embarrassed him a little to talk about how he'd watched her. Not that he'd done it, but that he'd revealed it to her. It seemed such a private thing. And by telling her, he'd opened himself up.

But Stella wasn't bothered. In fact, she seemed to like it. "This," she said finally, and Whit's heart began to pound. "Well, not this, exactly. Not the barn." She looked away then back again. "Leaving my father. Escape."

Whit swallowed. How was it possible that they wanted the same thing, but it wasn't the same at all? *Escape* meant something different for Stella than it did for Whit. She was running from something bad. Whit just wanted something better.

Stella grinned. "I guess I should have been more specific in my wish, huh. Then maybe you would have hidden me with the koala bears. Something from a whole other continent." She wrinkled her nose. "Not this ordinary old barn."

He shook his head. "You have no idea what you're saying."

"What? You don't like koala bears? But they're so cute and cuddly."

"Actually, they're not even bears. They're marsupials." Whit held his hands out in front of his stomach. "You know, the pouch? And they just *look* cute and cuddly. Really they're stubborn. Not to mention super hard to take care of. My mother kept a pair here at Meadowbrook Zoo for a few years. But it didn't work out."

"Maybe your mother just didn't try hard enough."

Whit threw his head back and laughed so loud that Penny mooed. He put his finger to his lips and worked to suppress his reaction. "It's not that," he said. If his mother ever failed, it wasn't for lack of trying. "It's just that to keep koalas, you really have to be able to grow eucalyptus trees on the zoo grounds. They're really finicky eaters."

"Well, what would you suggest then? What have

you got that's better than koalas?" She poked him in the chest. "And you can't say giraffes."

"Okay, well, you wouldn't want to stay with them, but what about the gorillas? You haven't really been behind the scenes at the zoo until you've visited the gorillas."

"I don't know." She pulled a cookie in the shape of a lion out of the box. "They're so . . . powerful."

"That's part of what's so cool about them. Just don't look them in the eye. They take it as a threat."

Stella crunched and swallowed. "What do they do? Pound their chests or something?"

"Sometimes. But mostly they spit."

"Like baseball players spit?"

Whit nodded. "Worse than that. And the keepers will make you take off your necktie or scarf. It could be real dangerous if one of the gorillas got hold of something tied around a person's neck."

Stella was quiet for a minute, then she wiggled the flashlight so that it made squiggly lines of light. "You know what's weird? There are all these rules for people to be around animals. But, for people? The school has a guidance counselor, but mostly she just tells us stuff about not bullying and not cheating and stuff about how to get along with other kids. No one tells you how to deal with parents. Like what to do when they yell. Or at what point *they* might be dangerous."

She sounded so serious, it gave Whit a funny feeling in his stomach. "Parents are way harder than chimps. That's for sure. With chimps, all you've got to do is give them a piece of sugarless cinnamon gum. Solves everything."

She laughed, and he thought it was the best animal sound of them all. As a quiet settled over the barn, Whit checked his watch. "Listen, Stella. This is only temporary, okay? After tonight, we've got to find somewhere else for you to stay."

She rolled the flashlight in her palm. "But where, Whit? There's nowhere for me to go."

He swallowed. He wasn't sure how much to say, because he'd thought about this. And he needed her to think about it, too. "What about Hugo? What about your cousins? Can't you and your mom go back to Mobile?"

She shot him an angry look and crossed her arms. But she didn't say a word.

"Come on, Stella . . . just think about it, okay? You can't stay here after tonight. There's just no way."

When she turned her back to him, he knew the conversation was over. He looked at his watch again. "Look, I've got to go back to the Lodge. Because of this whole Madagascar thing, my parents might actually be searching for me."

She still didn't speak.

He hated to leave her without smoothing things between them. But what else could he do? He sighed and got a picture of Tony at the table. And of his mother cooking supper with that big cast on her arm. They'd been through so much lately. No matter how mad he was about Madagascar and everything else, he couldn't just disappear the way Stella had. He couldn't do that to them. "I'll sneak out after they go to bed. But right now I've got to go back."

She was silent. Completely silent.

Whit placed the backpack on the floor in front of her. "If you get bored, there's plenty of stuff in here for you to do. And I'll be back in just a little while."

She tossed her hair back and finally spoke. "Fine, then. But I'm not going back in that hole. It's too creepy."

Whit peered into the darkness. It *was* creepy. "Okay, but you have to promise me you won't leave this store room. Stella, promise."

She smiled and held out her hand to shake on it. "Promise."

He took her hand. When he spoke again his voice was firm and insistent. "And don't make any noise. Gus has ears like a bat. Trust me, you don't want him poking around in here."

Stella took back her hand and saluted. "Yessir."

He grinned and backed out of the barn.

25 ✿ FIREWORKS

When he got back to the Lodge, Tony and Vivian were waiting for him at the table in the kitchen. The dishes had been cleared except for two wine glasses.

Probably they were going to tell him he had to go to Madagascar whether he liked it or not. And Whit wasn't at all sure how he should react. He was still mad, but not as mad as he was before. The whole conversation had just come as such a shock. And there was Stella to think about. He needed to tread carefully.

Tony cleared his throat and pulled out a chair for Whit. "Out a bit late, aren't you, son?"

"Just needed to blow off some steam, that's all."

Vivian took a sip of wine. "Well, there's something we need to talk to you about."

"Yep, Madagascar. I get it."

"Madagascar is one thing," Tony said, his voice thick with concern. "But there's something else."

Whit looked from one to the other. Whatever they had to tell him wasn't happy news. His heart began to beat faster.

"That girl you were with earlier," his mother said. "Stella." She stared at him hard. "When was the last time you saw her?"

Whit swallowed. Why were they asking about Stella? "I don't know. Why?"

Tony took a swig of wine then put his glass down. "She's missing. Her father was just on Channel 6. Said she's been missing for twelve hours."

Whit's eyes widened. Phil? On the news? "What else did they say?"

Vivian swirled her drink. "Oh, not much." Her voice had a hard edge to it. "Just something about how much they hated that she was missing, especially when she lived so close to a zoo that *still* hadn't recovered its snake." She lifted the glass to her lips and drained the remaining liquid. "Rodney just had to say 'more bad news for the zoo.' Like that helps anything." She sighed. "And, then her father said, and I quote: 'Zoos are an abomination and should be abolished.'"

Ouch, thought Whit. It sounded like Phil all right. Whit wondered now if his mother realized how ridiculous it was earlier when she'd offered Stella another free family membership. As if that would fix anything.

He needed to keep them talking about Phil so that they wouldn't ask him any more questions about Stella. He didn't want to lie to them if he could help it. "It's kind of funny, don't you think? I mean the guy hates zoos. And he lives right next to one."

"There's nothing funny about this, Whit." Vivian's face was blotchy. "A girl is missing. And the last place anyone saw her was at the zoo."

Whit scrambled to change the subject. "I thought we were going to talk about this stupid trip to Madagascar. Not some girl who's gone missing."

Tony scowled. "I thought you were friends, Whit."

There was that word again. *Friends.* He had to force back the smile that lifted his cheeks. Yep, he and Stella were friends. But to talk about her was to risk blowing her cover. She would be so mad if he revealed her. "I'll keep my eye out, okay? Now about Madagascar . . ."

"Yes," Vivian said, "about Madagascar. The tickets are bought. You're going." She paused. "And don't think we're finished discussing the missing girl. Because we're not."

The room was silent as Vivian's words floated around the room and settled square on Whit's shoulders.

Whit looked at Tony, but Tony just kept staring into his wineglass. Some father. He probably hadn't uttered a single word to Vivian about how Whit should stay.

Anger knotted Whit's stomach and made his fingers curl into fists. After all these years of trips to Tanzania and Costa Rica and Kenya, they had to go and pick *now* to include him. If ever there were an award for Terrible Timing, it would go to Tony and Vivian.

"It's not fair," Whit spit out the words, his anger billowing now to hurricane force. Even he knew he shouldn't be this mad about a trip to Madagascar, a trip that might even be fun if he let it. But that wasn't the point. The point was it was still his parents' thing. They were making him go on a trip he didn't care one thing about. Sure the lemurs were cute, and yes, they needed all the help they could get to prevent the species from extinction. But why did it have to involve him?

Whit seethed. "I wish I had never been born."

Tony snapped. "Don't say that, Whit. Just . . . don't."

"Don't stop him, Tony." Vivian waved her arms in the air. "Let him get it all out. How awful we are as parents. How mean and terrible and wicked." She laughed a bitter laugh. "It's true, isn't it? We never wanted—"

"Vivian, enough," Tony said, and reached for her arm. Then he looked at Whit, his eyes liquid with apology and regret. "She's just had a long day. What with the arm and all. . . . She doesn't know what she's saying."

Whit didn't believe that. And he knew just how that sentence must end. *We never wanted* you. "Well, I never wanted you, either." His chest burned, and he knew he should stop, but he couldn't. "It's no wonder the snake slithered away. And the zebra today. Even Stella." Whit swallowed. "They're all trying to get away from *you.*"

It was as if all the air got sucked out of the room. Whit couldn't have stunned them more if he'd hit them.

Whit opened his mouth to speak, to explain, to maybe even take it back. But a flash of light through the window distracted them all.

"It's probably some fool putting up fireworks," Tony said.

Whit shook his head and walked toward the window, his parents right behind him.

As he pulled the curtain back, he gasped.

It wasn't fireworks. It was *fire*.

26 ❧ CODE RED

Whit's chest got so tight he couldn't breathe. The flames were coming from the barn. "Call 9-1-1! There's a fire in the zoo!"

Vivian pressed her face against the window. "Fire? Are you sure?"

Whit nodded and he choked back tears. An image of Stella came into his mind, then an image of her hand closing around Phil's lighter. Why hadn't he told her about the hay, how flammable it is? When he brought her the flashlight, why hadn't he warned her not to use the lighter?

Vivian's yanked her walkie-talkie out of its holster. "Code Red. Alert. Code Red." Not once in Whit's memory had they used that code, but everyone knew *red* meant fire. And even though it was in the middle of the night, the keepers would want to know. The entire zoo had practiced the monthly fire drill just two days ago.

"Yes, that's right," Tony said into the phone, and looked out the window. "The Meadowbrook Zoo. Fire looks to be in the direction of the barn, but I can't be sure from this distance."

Vivian moaned, "No, no, no. This can't be happening!"

Whit moaned, too. He should tell them about Stella. He knew he should. But his throat was so tight no words would come out.

Tony placed his hand over the receiver and spoke to Vivian. "It's the drought. The operator says fires have been popping up all over the state in the past week."

Vivian pressed the button on the walkie-talkie. "Gus. Gus. Come in Gus."

Whit held his breath.

When no answer came, Vivian cradled her cast and slipped on her shoes. "I'm going down there. I've got to see what's going on."

Whit bolted for the door. His mother wasn't the only one who needed to see what was happening.

Tony blocked the doorway. "Whit, Vivian. Wait!" He held his hand over the receiver again. "Three different fire crews are on their way. The operator said we shouldn't get too close. And it wouldn't hurt to wet down the yard all around the Lodge to prevent spread of the fire in this direction."

Panic pitched Whit's voice higher than usual. "But what about the animals? We've got to get them out of there!"

He swallowed. *What about Stella?*

Thank goodness he hadn't locked her in the hole. She'd get out because she was smart and capable. But the barn animals, they were a different story. They needed help.

Tony slammed down the phone and grabbed Whit's arm. "Come on. Help me with the hoses."

Whit followed Tony out the door as two fire trucks charged through the empty parking lot, their sirens wailing. The red and white lights surged across the sky, making the Education Building look like something out of a scary movie. Several cars followed behind the engines, some of them police, some of them vehicles Whit recognized as belonging to animal keepers. The troops had arrived.

Whit dropped the hose. "I'm going down there, Dad. They might need help."

"Son, no! It's not safe."

But Whit didn't listen. He ran as fast as he could. He needed to see Stella. He had to know for sure that she was okay.

The parking lot seethed with activity as two more fire crews filed in and began to battle the blaze. Beads of sweat popped out on Whit's forehead and his eyes began to burn. The air closer to the fire was hot and heavy, and breathing took actual effort.

Whit stopped when he reached the barricade police had erected in front of the Education Building and around the edge of the parking lot. A policeman shouted through a megaphone. "For your own safety, do not cross this line."

Smoke billowed above the flames, and the odor enveloped him. It wasn't just smoke, but rubber and wood and something else. Whit clamped a hand over his nose and mouth so he wouldn't gag. He gave his stomach a few seconds to settle then took a step forward.

And he wasn't the only one. Whit recognized the barn keepers and followed suit as they scrambled around the tail end of the barricade. There wasn't a thing that would make keepers stay away from their charges when they were in danger. Not even police.

Whit couldn't believe how intense the flames were. Or how far beyond the barn the fire had spread. There were shouts and blasts of water and the crackle of dry wood being consumed by fire.

It was impossible to get any closer to the barn. It was already just a carcass now as fire fighters turned their hoses toward the carousel and the Education Building.

The keepers called for the animals. "Penny!"

Whit held his arm over his nose as he got as close to the flames as he could. "Please, Stella! It's me, Whit!"

Whit circled what was left of the building. She *had* to have gotten out. She just had to.

The firefighter's megaphone boomed. "Stay away from the buildings. I repeat. Stay away. Or we will be forced to lock you in a patrol car."

Whit sank to his knees beside the keepers. "Did any of them get out? Penny or the chickens or any of them?"

The bearded one who just hours before had propped the animal charts on his hip shook his head. "Dunno, kid."

Whit knew what his mother would say. At least it was a night when there weren't any guests. She would totally play up the fact that the fire was at night, not the worst-case scenario.

Except there *was* a guest. A girl with long brown hair. One the police were supposed to be looking for, but probably had completely forgotten in the midst of the fire.

"Stella," Whit whispered, his voice cracking. "Where are you?"

He knew he should tell someone she had been in there. But he didn't know who to tell. Or how.

He shook his head. He had to trust that she would be okay. Because he knew the whole point was for her to hide, to run away like Hugo. A true friend wouldn't blow her cover.

27 ✻ INDEPENDENCE DAY

Hours passed before the fire was completely extinguished. Whit's muscles were wooden from the endless waiting. He just wanted it to be over. He wanted to see Stella okay and in one piece.

The big trucks pulled out of the parking lot as one of the officers assembled a search team. Now that the blaze was out, the team could go in and search the wreckage to determine what caused the fire and also to find out the extent of the damages. Whit knew this was a fancy way of saying "see what died." And he knew he needed to tell them about Stella. He had waited long enough.

As the team went in, Vivian stood outside the barricade. She stared at the remains of the building, her sweatpants dragging on the ground and her arm drawn up in the sling. Whit fought the urge to throw his arm around her. He knew she wouldn't like it, not in this situation, not when things looked so bleak. "I'm sorry," he said. As he said the words, he realized he could be talking about any number of things—the fire, the fight about the trip to Madagascar, Stella. He needed to be more specific.

Before he could explain, his mother's voice came in a whisper. "Me, too, Whit." She put her hand on his shoulder. "Happy Independence Day."

Whit stalled. He didn't want to kill the moment. It was so rare for his mother to be so quiet, so still. "Will you close the zoo?"

"Don't have any choice. The police said we have to, at least until the investigation is finished." She pressed her good palm against her forehead. Whit knew the timing couldn't be any worse. They wouldn't be breaking any Fourth of July attendance records this year. "And we'll have to postpone our trip to Madagascar," she continued. "There's no way we can leave the zoo now. Not until we can get the barn rebuilt."

Whit's stomach clutched. His brain chanted *Stella, Stella*, but the words just would not come out of his mouth. "Where will we put the animals?" Relocation, even on a temporary basis, made everyone's jobs more difficult.

"What animals, Whit? What animals are you talking about? Because I think the search team would have shouted if there were any signs of life. It's way too quiet."

His heart was hard and tight, like a chestnut. He didn't want Penny to be dead. Penny, or the pigs, or the chickens.

Vivian shook her head. "Now the investigators are just trying to determine what started the fire."

"But I thought it was just the drought. Maybe some fireworks or something."

"Could be." His mother wiped her nose. "The officers want to rule out arson. They're concerned because of what the girl—Stella—what her father said on TV about wanting the zoo abolished."

Whit grabbed her arm and looked her in the eye. "Mom, I have to tell you something. Please."

She stood her ground. "It can't wait?"

He shook his head. "I should have told you before." He pushed the tears back and made himself look her in the eye. It was so much bigger than the missing snake and the trip to Madagascar.

"Tell me now," she said.

Whit's breath came in spurts. He didn't know how else to say it, except to just say it. "My friend—Stella." He swallowed back the lump in his throat. "Stella Taylor. She was here. Tonight. In the barn."

28 ❋ THE WINDOW

It took all of three seconds for Vivian to flag down one of the officers *and* put out a Joe DiMaggio on her walkie-talkie. Not for an escaped animal this time. For Stella.

Once inside the house, Whit told her about the lighter, too. It was as if he couldn't stop the words now that he'd finally found them. He had to tell her everything.

When he was done, she sank into the nearest kitchen chair. "Good Lord, Whit! What were you doing in the barn? And what was she doing with a lighter?"

Whit pressed his fingers against his temples. He didn't know how much to tell her. "It's Phil's. Her dad. He's a smoker. She took it from him because she was mad. Then she gave it to me, and I gave it back. It's just a lighter, Mom. It may not have anything to do with anything."

"Whit, don't you get it? I don't care about the lighter. I care about the *girl*. What if she's still in the barn?" Her eyes got shiny. "With Penny?"

Whit shook his head. "She's not. She's too smart for that." Just saying the words made him feel more confident. "Besides, she's like hard-wired for escape. There's just no way she didn't get out."

Vivian sat down with a heavy sigh. "I can't talk anymore, Whit. It's too much." She cradled her broken arm and put her head on the table.

Whit sat down, too, but when his mother started to sob, he couldn't stay still.

He paced instead. There was too much going on inside him, too much worry, too much adrenaline pumping. He had to keep moving. And after a few minutes he couldn't stand the crying anymore. The worst part was not knowing what to do.

"I'll be in my room," he said, and placed a hand on her shoulder. "Let me know if you hear anything."

Whit closed the door and sat on his bed. Everything was just as he'd left it: the walls, the floor, the window. The stars glowed softly, same as they always had.

He'd wanted to show the stars to Stella. He'd wanted to bring her to his room the same way she had brought him to hers. He wasn't sure now if that would ever happen.

Whit stretched across the bed and rubbed his eyes. What if he never saw the Bird Girl again? He was so sleepy he could hardly keep his eyelids up. But he was far too pent up with worry for sleep. It was the not knowing that made his whole body tense.

He wondered if this was what it was like for animals in the wild. This restlessness. He bet they were hardly ever fully asleep. It was too risky.

When Whit turned his head toward the window, something caught his eye. He jerked himself off the bed, heart pounding.

It was a face. *Stella*'s face!

She was alive! The window pushed open with hardly any trouble at all, and she climbed through. "Stella, thank God!"

"You missed me?" When she pushed her hair back, her fingers left ashy smudges on her face. He quickly scanned her body for other evidence of the fire.

"Are you okay? My mom just called the police. They think you're still in there!"

"You told them?" Her voice was small, disappointed.

"Stella, I had to. You were on the news! Phil . . . he was on the news, too."

She sank onto the bed and covered her face with her hands.

He sat beside her. When he threw an arm around her, he could feel her shoulders trembling. "It's going to be okay." He patted her back. "I'm sorry, but I had to tell them." He gripped her arm. "Stella, what if you had died? I mean, what if you hadn't gotten out?"

She sobbed. "Now what am I going to do?"

Whit didn't have an answer so he just kept patting her back.

She swallowed and wiped her eyes. "It was so scary! I was in that closet, and I thought, no one will see the light in here. Not Gus, not you, no one." She swallowed hard. "And when I flipped the switch, there was a pop. Then it started to smoke. Next thing I knew it was burning." She sniffled. "The smell was so awful. I was afraid I would choke. I got out of there as fast as I could."

It was scary enough watching it from a distance, thought Whit.

"I couldn't even think," she continued. "By the

time I remembered the animals, how I should let them out, the fire engines were already rolling in, Whit. It happened so fast . . . there wasn't time."

He swallowed hard. "I'm just glad you're okay."

She tucked her hair behind her ear. "You were worried?"

"Yep, I was worried. Of course."

She rubbed her forehead, then grabbed his hands. "Come with me, Whit. This is our chance. You know, to escape."

She was so close Whit could see tiny beads of sweat across the bridge of her nose. And her eyes were bright as ever. "What are you talking about?"

"You know. How you don't like the zoo. And I hate my life. Let's leave them. Forget Hugo's plan. I can't wait for that anymore. Things are never going to get better. My father—he's never going to get better." She chewed her lip. "Let's go somewhere and live all by ourselves. In the wild." She squeezed his hands. "It'll be great, you'll see."

It sounded so good. Just like when the animal rights people came around with their picket signs: FREE THE ANIMALS and PUT THEM BACK IN THE WILD. But it wasn't as easy as that. "Stella, that's crazy.

We're only eleven years old. Where would we live? Who would take care of us?"

"We'd figure it out. We'd be free."

Whit shook his head. For many of the animals in the zoo, freedom meant death. He shook his head again. Truth was, he didn't really want to leave the zoo. If Stella had taught him anything, it was that the zoo is a pretty cool place to be.

He couldn't meet her eyes. And he couldn't leave. Not like this. "I can't." His situation wasn't like Stella's. His parents cared enough about him to give him Ms. Connie and "socialization." It wasn't everything he wanted, but it wasn't smoke and yelling and stray gunshots.

"Can't, or won't?"

"Both, Stella." He wanted to explain his revelation, but he didn't know how to do that without making her feel even worse. "It's not smart. I mean just imagine your mother. She would go crazy if you disappeared. She would go nuts."

"She'd get over it."

Whit sighed. She didn't even know what she was saying. "No she wouldn't, Stella. You don't get over something like that."

"So, what, you're telling me *no*?"

He made himself look her in the eye. This time there was no blush, no nervousness. He had never been so sure of anything in his life. "I'm not running away."

"Then I'll go by myself."

She scrambled out of the window like she made fast escapes every day. Whit leaned out of the window as she disappeared into the forest. "Stella, no!"

When she didn't turn, he pulled himself back in. He couldn't let her do this. It wasn't safe. It wasn't right.

"Mom," he called, and raced to the kitchen. "It's Stella. She was just here. At my bedroom window." He picked up her walkie-talkie. "Joe DiMaggio found. Stella Taylor in woods near Lodge. Repeat, Stella Taylor in woods near Lodge. Recovery team needed."

29 ✳ THE NOTE

The police picked up Stella within minutes of the call. Whit wasn't there when it happened, but he did see it on Channel 6. Mrs. Taylor was there, too, trapped beside Stella on that tiny TV screen. Rodney didn't say *"awesome"* or *"cool"* or any other words like them. His eyes drooped and his voice wavered, as if he really did love the zoo and was sorry to be giving such a report. Whit decided he liked Rodney better this way.

And he knew he'd done the right thing. As much as it had killed him to turn Stella in, to do the exact opposite of what she wanted, he knew he'd done the right thing.

Still, Whit wanted to apologize to her, to explain why he couldn't let her escape, why he couldn't escape *with* her, why he ultimately chose his parents and the zoo. So the next day, after he'd slept past noon, he hiked through the Botanical Gardens to talk to her.

The air smelled of smoke the whole way over. No telling how long the odor would linger. As if the charred remains of the barn weren't enough of a reminder.

When he arrived at Stella's back door, it was like going back in time to the day when they took Phil's gun. Poppy strained on his chain, tail wagging its greeting. Whit knocked even though the blinds were drawn and hoped someone would answer.

No one came to Stella's door. But a crowd of kids tumbled out of Juan Carlos's apartment. Whit greeted them and watched as his sister Carmen turned on the sprinkler. "Five minutes," Juan Carlos shouted from the doorway. "Mom said because of the drought we can only run the water for five minutes!"

Whit grinned at Juan Carlos, and the other boy came down and gave him a high five. The yo-yo was mysteriously missing. "Where's Fred?" Whit asked.

Juan Carlos dipped his hand in his pocket. "Right here." He spun the yo-yo down like a pro.

"What about Stella? Any idea where she is?"

"You won't believe this, but I saw Mrs. Taylor leaving with Stella this morning. And for once Phil wasn't in the car."

Whit stepped back. "What do you mean he wasn't there? Where was he?"

"Stella didn't say exactly. All she said was that she and her mother were going to Mobile. That Hugo was waiting for them."

"Wow." Whit grinned. "So Mrs. Taylor actually left Phil." It was the best news Whit had heard in days.

Juan Carlos lifted his eyebrows. "Not exactly. Mr. Taylor is at a treatment center, for the pain pills and everything. My mom said that if he gets better, they might be able to try again. To be a family. We just don't know."

"But what about the gun? Did Phil ever find out we were the ones who took it?"

Juan Carlos did a trick move with Fred that Whit didn't recognize. "Mr. Taylor was so mad when he found out it was missing." He shook his head. "My mom had to call the police. Again. It was pretty bad. But the police said to let them handle it. So that's what we did. "

"And now they're all gone. Like, for good." Whit shoved his hands in his pockets to fight off the chill that shot from his head all the way to his toes. "Wow."

As Juan Carlos nodded, he flexed his finger to draw Fred back up the string.

"Wow," Whit said again. Mobile was so far away. And he hadn't had a chance to give Stella a proper goodbye.

Nope, the last time they were together, he'd turned her in. She probably hated him for it.

If only he could get in touch with her. "Juan Carlos, would you do me a favor?"

"Depends on what is is." He nodded his head toward Stella's door.

Whit sliced the air with his hands. "No more guns for me. Got a pencil and some paper?"

When Juan Carlos returned, Whit scratched out a quick note to Stella. He apologized first. Then he asked her about her life in Mobile. He invited her to write to him, if she wanted to.

He wanted to tell her about the barn animals lost in the fire. About Penny and the pigs, how all of them were found in the wreckage. Not burned, but dead from asphyxiation. All that smoke caught in a closed space—Doc said it was a blessing, really. That at least they never had to feel the flames.

But it seemed like an awful thing to write in a letter. So he just wrote about the good stuff instead. About Ferdinand waddling out of the woods after the fire, his feathers spread wide. As if to say, "All is not lost! I'm alive!"

When he was finished, he folded the letter in thirds. "Now all I need is her address. Think your mom has it?"

Juan Carlos sent Fred spinning with the flick of a finger. "No problem."

30 ✳ THE BIRD GIRL

By the first of August, work was underway to build a new barn, along with a bigger and better farm exhibit. One with the most advanced electrical system available. In fact, donations arrived in envelopes every single day, thanks to all the guests who loved the barn. Whit had even read a few of the letters while his mother was busy meeting with corporate sponsors and setting up various fund-raisers.

There wasn't any doubt in Whit's mind that the zoo would recover, same as it always did. He would recover, too, although he sure missed Stella.

A week later, on the second Monday of the month, it began to rain. It rained for three days straight. According to Channel 6, the storm brought in seven inches of rain in some places. With all the guests snug in their homes and offices, the animals stayed in their huddles while keepers worked overtime to keep the enclosures clean.

Was it raining in Mobile? Whit sat at the breakfast table and wondered what Stella was doing, how she was spending her time now that she wasn't at the zoo drawing birds.

"Whit?" his mother said, coming in with a stack of papers. "How close are you to finishing your summer schoolwork?"

Whit took another bite of a banana, chewed and swallowed. He hadn't even thought about the field study in weeks. "I've got till the end of August, right?"

Vivian pulled out the chair next to Whit. "Not this year." She pushed the papers toward him.

Whit gasped as he read the top of the page. "Registration Packet: Meadowbrook Middle School."

"No way."

Vivian nodded. "I picked it up on the drive back from my checkup." She lifted her purple cast. "If you want to give it a try, classes start two weeks from Tuesday. But I have to give them all your school records. Which means you've got to finish up with all your work."

Whit could feel a lump growing in his throat. For

a long moment he couldn't speak. He'd thought it was huge when she'd canceled the trip to Madagascar. But even that was nothing compared to this. Regular school, just like he wanted! And she was completely focused on *him*, her son. His mother was paying attention.

Whit felt lighter than cotton candy, like he just might melt right there. "Thanks, Mom."

She shook her head. "We should have done it a long time ago. I'm sorry it took us so long to realize the zoo isn't the best place for you."

Whit threw his arms around her shoulders and hugged her hard, careful not to bump her cast. When she hugged him back, he sank into her a little. From now on he was going to try harder to talk to her. He wasn't going to let himself be forgotten. He was going to tell her stuff, important stuff. The way Juan Carlos did with his mom.

As he crossed the parking lot from the Lodge to the zoo entrance, he smiled. It really was a great zoo. At his secret spot in the shadows of the Reptile House, he looked around the place with a feeling of pride. It had been so much fun showing the zoo to Stella.

He watched a man with a toddler on his shoulders settle onto the wall of the Turtle Pond and point at the turtles. It wasn't really the zoo that was the problem. It just wasn't the right fit for Whit. He needed *more*.

As the father and son ambled away, Whit walked out to the bench in front of Flamingo Island. He sat in the same spot Stella always did and pulled out his digital recorder. "Subject gone for weeks now. Flamingos miss her. Turtles miss her." Whit let off the button and swallowed before beginning again. "But no one—no one—misses the Bird Girl more than me."

Then Whit told the digital recorder everything he'd been wanting to say about Stella, about the fire and the last time he saw her at his bedroom window. Instead of just reporting the actions, he talked about his feelings, too. How hard it was, and how much he missed his friend. "And that concludes my summer field study," he said, and set the recorder on the bench.

It was sure going to be strange without Ms. Connie coming to teach him three times a week. But it was time. Even she knew that. And she said as much when he turned in his field study and told her the news.

"A human, huh?" She smiled. "Good choice."

"Nothing against you, Ms. Connie. You know that, right?"

She patted his back. "Of course I do, Whit. You've

been a pleasure—an absolute pleasure—to teach. And you're going to do great in middle school. Girls love boys who like animals."

A blush crept up Whit's neck as he thanked her and promised to keep her posted.

"Now if we could just convince your parents to get you a cell phone. Then you could just text me, and I wouldn't have to worry."

He handed her the media card from his digital recorder, then threw his arms around her with an abandon he hadn't experienced since he was four. Who would he be, if not for Ms. Connie?

She turned her face away, but Whit could still see her dab at the corners of her eyes. "There's one more thing I need to tell you, Whit. In case you were wondering."

He squinted against the sun. "Okay."

"It's about that trip to Madagascar. It wasn't just about the lemurs." She took a deep breath. "Your mother wanted so much for it to be a surprise. Do you remember that unit we did on Africa? How we went to the drugstore for a mock passport?"

Whit nodded, remembering the goofy face he'd made for the camera.

"Well, that was real, Whit. That passport was real. Your mother was planning that trip for a long time." She paused. "And do you remember going to the doctor for your 'sixth grade shots'? Your mother asked them to add in a couple of shots for going to Africa. For malaria and tetanus."

He rubbed the top of his arm, remembering. His mouth was dry. Was it possible his mother had been paying attention and he just hadn't noticed? He shook his head. Maybe paying attention was something they *both* needed to work on.

Ms. Connie squeezed his shoulder. "And now, instead of Madagascar, you're ready for a whole new adventure."

He grinned. Middle school! He'd take it over Madagascar any day. And he was determined that things were going to be different now. He was done with just watching. From now on, he planned to spend more time *doing*. And not just any old thing, or just because his parents told him to do it. From now on, he wasn't going to wait around the zoo for something like the Bird Girl to happen. He was going to *make* things happen. And he was going to ask his parents for what he needed instead of waiting for them to figure it out.

He flipped the collar of his regulation zoo shirt. Starting with his clothes. No more green, no more khaki pants. And he needed some cool shoes. He slid the digital recorder into his pocket and went to find his mother.

On the first day of school, Whit got dressed in the new jeans and stylish sneakers Juan Carlos had helped him pick out, and his mother drove him out of the zoo gates to Meadowbrook Middle School where a banner above the carport said, "Welcome to a Great New School Year!"

Vivian steered the car in a parking space and Whit opened the door. He couldn't believe it. Finally, it was here: his first day at public school.

"Whit, wait," his mother said. Whit turned back to her and hoped she wasn't going to smooth down his hair or kiss him or some other equally embarrassing gesture. It wasn't something she'd ever done before but ever since the fire she'd been a little different. "Here," she said. "I found it when I checked the mailbox this morning."

Whit crinkled his brow and reached for the envelope in her outstretched hand. "What is it?"

"See for yourself." She looked through the front windshield to give him some privacy.

The address was written in colored pencil. Realization dawned in Whit's mind, and his fingers shook as he fumbled with the seal. When the opening was large enough, he pulled out a single sheet of paper. His heart hammered in his chest as he unfolded it.

Then, when he saw what was there, his nose began to sting the way it did before tears.

It was a drawing of a peacock. And of a boy that looked an awful lot like Whit. He had light yellow hair and everything.

Whit looked more closely. At the bottom it was labeled "Ferdinand and Whit, A Cowboy Needs a ~~Horse~~ Peacock??" Then there was another line. "Thanks for everything. You're a true friend. Love, Bird Girl."

Whit leaned his head against the back of the seat and smiled. Then he pressed the corners of his eyes and a laugh burbled out of his throat. They'd had so much fun with that whole Billy the Kid act.

She wasn't mad. She was safe and happy. And free.

She was the Bird Girl. And someday he would see her again—he just didn't know when.

Meanwhile, the sidewalk in front of the school

swarmed with students. One of them was Juan Carlos. He gave a nod when he saw Whit, and motioned for him to hurry up and join them. Whit checked his watch: 7:45. Just like they'd planned when Juan Carlos agreed to educate him on a whole new set of rules— the *non*-zoo rules.

"Guess I should go," he said to his mother.

Vivian smiled. "See you at three o'clock."

The door made a solid sound as it closed behind him. As Whit joined Juan Carlos and two other guys he recognized from that day at the zoo, he threw his shoulders back and adjusted the straps on his backpack. He was surrounded by kids his own age. Kids he would see every single school day. Kids he might eventually call *friends*.

Finally he felt like the right species. In exactly the right spot.

ACKNOWLEDGMENTS

Heartfelt thanks to zoo people everywhere who devote so much time and energy to education and to the preservation of animal species. You are an endless source of inspiration and enjoyment in my life.

To Rosemary Stimola, thank you for believing in this story. To the entire staff at Roaring Brook Press, especially Nancy Mercado, thank you for your tender care and enormous enthusiasm. And to Stephanie Graegin, thanks for your gorgeous illustrations. You've charmed Whit and the Bird Girl to tender life.

Deepest thanks to four very special readers whose invaluable feedback at crucial times made this book so much richer and more textured: Stacey Barney, Kathy Erskine, Summer Laurie, and Stephanie Shaw. To Jerri Beck, thanks for double-checking my zoo facts. Special thanks to Mrs. Young's Yacht Club of Inverness Elementary School, 2009–10: You are inside these pages.

The journey would be nothing without the loved ones who share the path: my sister, Lynn Baker, who has given me a gift subscription to *Writers Digest* for as long as I can remember and listens in those crazy-writer-lady moments when I need her the most; Pat Weaver, whose friendship is a great blessing in my life; little brother MicaJon Dykes who understands and shares the creative struggle; my "Birmingham parents," Jim & Liz Reed; and two very special nephews, Alex and Matt Baker, and niece JuliAnna Dykes—young writers, all. Thanks for being my best cheerleaders!

Thanks also to Papa, who always asks how my writing life is progressing—and offers wonderful advice and suggestions; to Mama, who thinks all my ideas are brilliant, even the ones that really aren't; to Daniel, who inspires peace and confidence; to Andrew, without whom there would be no Whit; to Eric, the best assistant ever! And most especially, to Paul: Thank you for the days and nights. It's A Wonderful Life.